Paris

By
Avery Gale

PARIS
Copyright © 2019 by Avery Gale
ISBN: 978-1-944472-79-5
Print Edition

PUBLISHER
Avery Gale
averygale.com

Cover Design by Jess Buffett at Sinfully Sweet Designs
Editing by Sandy Ebel at Personal Touch Editing
Proofreading and Second Edits by Karen Bailey

The Adlers

The siblings. Their occupations and ages at the beginning of the series:

Austin – 31 – CEO of the family oil conglomerate based in Austin, TX. Married to magical, Charlotte, who is expecting at the end of Austin's book.

Asia – 30 – Ruthless legal eagle for the family business. Shifter.

Bronx – 29 – Owns a string of car dealerships in partnership with brother, Cleveland.

Cleveland – 28 – Race car driver.

Brooklyn – 27 – Retrieval expert for big insurance companies. Semi-retired in subsequent books. Security consultant. Married to Luke Grayson, lives in New Mexico.

Catalina – 26 – Freelance intelligent agent, working with the CIA, MI6, Mossad, and others. Travels the world as a successful jewelry designer.

Israel – 25 – Security expert and tracker.

Kensington – 24 – Actor.

London – 23 – Chemist/Researcher. Married to shifters, Elijah & Evan Monroe, lives outside Boston.

Paris – 22 – Recent College Graduate.

Watch this page for updates in subsequent books in this series.

Chapter One

*F*UCKITY *FUCK.* PARIS Adler felt like she'd replaced one stalker with another. For Goddess' sake, what kind of cop stood in the shadows watching a woman swim naked? Mentally rolling her eyes, Paris had to admit there were several significant differences between the man who'd sent her life in California spiraling out of control and the hot Sheriff currently standing in the shadows, shrouded in semi-darkness. *Get it together, Paris. Real stalker versus cop stalker.* Giving herself a mental forehead slap, Paris decided it was entirely possible she was losing her mind. *I'm going to end up in some fancy sanitarium, eating checkers and watching classic movies all day if I don't yank my head out of my backside.*

The whole situation in California was a textbook case of what, Paris later learned, was referred to as *victim grooming.* The man and the fiasco she'd run from on the west coast had snuck up on her. Her friendship with David Lamb had been easy—too easy as it turned out. He'd slipped past her well-honed defenses, befriending her their freshman year. David had been her biggest supporter and the shoulder she cried on when her life started spiraling out of control her senior year. *Yeah, no irony there!*

Agreeing to house-sit for her sister, London, and her

two husbands, Elijah and Evan Monroe, while they were on their honeymoon had been an easy yes. As far as her family knew, she was on a short break, awaiting graduation when, in fact, she was finished with school and had already been presented her diploma. There wasn't a chance in hell she was going back to California for a ceremony that would put her anywhere near her former friend. Hell, his messages—and she'd received a lot of them—had sworn he would kill her before he let her go.

For the first time since she dove naked into the Monroe's sheltered pool, Paris was so distracted, she lost the rhythm of her stroke. Recovering quickly, she flipped in time to turn and shove off the wall into another lap. The man lurking in the dark watched her with such intensity, it radiated off him in waves. She hadn't realized he was close until she'd already stripped, diving cleanly into the refreshing water.

All she'd wanted to do was push her body to the point of exhaustion, hoping her mind would follow suit and she could finally sleep without the nightmares that had returned after her trip to the Caribbean. Now, she had a new stalker to contend with, and if she wasn't careful, Sheriff Stone could do more damage to her heart than David. The fear and betrayal she'd felt over the past year were devastating but losing her best friend had crushed her. Fucking hell, she'd better pay attention, or she was going to swim into the damned wall.

Oh yeah, I'm sure Sheriff Stone will be monumentally impressed if you plow headfirst into the concrete wall of the pool.

He'd been her assigned bodyguard during the Monroe's wedding week. Paris honestly believed Sheriff Stone had tried to blend into the background, but when you are nearly seven frick-fracking feet tall, blending is damned difficult. Their last night in the Caribbean, her future sister-in-law had nearly been kidnapped right out from under their noses. Mr. I'm the Boss of You standing like a damned sentinel at the end of the pool had ordered her to stay with London. Of course, Paris being Paris meant she'd promptly done the exact opposite... and the good sheriff had been incensed. She wasn't sure what he'd been angrier about—that she'd put herself in danger or because she'd blatantly ignored his edict. Damn it all to hell, as the youngest of ten, she'd been bossed around her entire life, and *she was just fucking over it*.

She'd once again taken a mental road trip, losing herself in her musings and wondering where the world's hottest ass had gone, when she was unceremoniously yanked from the water.

"What the fuck? You can't just yank me out of the water like an errant child." Fuck a one-legged duck, she was naked, dripping wet, and so mad she could barely see straight. Swiping long blonde strands of hair from her eyes, Paris glared at the sheriff. She was already teetering on an emotional edge, the strain of the past several months was finally catching up with her. Damn, it frosted her cookies to admit it, but the simple truth was, if she didn't manage to get some blessed sleep, she was going to implode.

Going to the island resort ahead of her family to make sure everything was arranged to her sister's liking had been both a blessing and a curse. She'd appreciated getting out of the country and knowing she was safe. Her sister, Brooklyn's fiancé, Luke Grayson, wasn't the only one who could do research. She'd quickly discovered the resort hosting the wedding was owned and operated by a former Special Agent. The entire facility was described in reviews as a virtual fortress, making her feel safe for the first time in over a year.

Shaking her head, trying to refocus on the man whose monster mitt was wrapped around her bicep, Paris tried to push back the memory of how that same hand had felt slapping her bare ass, but her libido wasn't cooperating. When he'd pulled her over his lap, she'd quickly discovered the man wasn't just freaking tall... he was big everywhere. Feeling his enormous and rock-hard cock pressing against her side, combined with the heated slaps to her ass cheeks had been enough to send her sailing over the edge into the most intense orgasm of her life.

Sneaking out after Sheriff Stone was asleep hadn't been easy since they were sharing a villa. Damn her family for believing she needed a bodyguard. Her sisters better fucking stop all their daredevil bullshit because Paris was tired of having a net dropped over her when one of them stirred up some kind of trouble. Every time there was a threat to one of the Adler women, they were all suddenly on lock-down. But Paris had been so embarrassed by her explosive reaction to the spanking, she'd pulled out all the stops to ensure she traveled alone back Boston.

Hell, she hadn't left the secured compound of Evan Monroe's medical facility since she'd arrived a week ago. She'd even used the underground tunnel connecting the home Evan lived in before mating with London to the family's palatial residence next door. A large part of the neighboring mansion was used by pack members, including the commercially equipped kitchen, an Olympic sized pool, and a wide array of offices. The rest of the impressive structure was the private residence of the pack's Alphas, Elijah and Dr. Evan Monroe, and their new mate, Paris' sister, London.

London had laughed when she'd told Paris how she'd gotten lost in her new home one night after taking a wrong turn. The irony of the situation couldn't be overstated since London Adler was one of the most gifted medical researchers in the world. Her discoveries were going to change the face of medicine forever and knowing the woman with a mind that processed information at the speed of light had gotten lost in her own home was one of the funniest things Paris had heard in a very long time.

Damn it, Paris, pull your head out of your ass and focus.

"WE NEED TO have a chat, Paris." Trinity Stone saw her eyes widen in surprise when he used her given name. He had a variety of pet names for her, some of them less flattering than others. Smiling to himself, Trinity took a few seconds to savor the moment—he knew Paris Adler well enough to feel certain rendering her momentary speechless was a sweet victory, but would undoubtedly be fleeting.

"You could have just called." Her mutinous tone might have been amusing if her body wasn't playing from an entirely different sheet of music. *And a sweet song, it is.* The scent of her arousal was already masking the burning stench of the chlorine. The reminder of how his fingers had carried the sweet aroma of her cream, after she'd come for him after four swats, sent a damn-bursting surge of blood to his already aching cock. *Fuck me, she is spectacular; it should be a fucking crime to wrap her in a towel.* He'd pulled a bath sheet from the nearby warmer, but he was damned hesitant to use it, preferring the unobstructed view of the sex goddess standing before him.

"Are you sure this is the way you want this to go, Beautiful? Hell, I'd like nothing better than to keep you stark naked while we talk—I assure you, the view is spectacular." His eyes moved over the body he was sure would taste every bit as sweet as it looked. Trinity kept his eyes moving in a sensual slide he hoped she felt to the depths of her soul.

"Baby, the moonlight loves you. It highlights your per-fectly formed breasts, drawing my eyes to the beads of water racing to their sweet tips. Watching those drops let go of your candy-pink nipples might just become my new favorite pastime." *Truer words have never been spoken. When she finally belongs to me, I may keep her naked all the time.*

Trinity knew the first time he met wild child Paris Ad-ler, she belonged to him. He'd stopped the little hellion for speeding and felt his knees weaken when she'd rolled down the window of her sporty rental. The phony look of innocence on her heart-shaped face had almost made him burst out laughing. Trinity hadn't needed a mirror to know his nostrils flared as the scent of his mate reached out, the addictive aroma's tentacles wrapping themselves around his heart. He'd been determined to hold back his desire until he was confident she was ready for what a relation-ship with him would entail. *Who am I kidding? I'm not that*

fucking righteous—I'd just been afraid I'd scare her off. Every-
thing about this woman makes me want to push myself balls deep
and never leave her sweet heat.

"Tell me about David Lamb, Paris." Trinity felt a tidal wave of emotion slam into him like a tsunami. A virtual playbook of mixed reactions moved over her expressive face. Trin knew the youngest Adler was close to losing her battle with an internal flight or fight response, finely honed by generations of shifters who preceded her. Softening his stance and hoping his voice would reflect his worry, he continued, "Talk to me, sweetheart."

As the moon peeked out from behind a cloud, Trin could see the dark circles under her ocean-blue eyes and wondered if fear of her damned stalker was keeping her from sleeping. *Baby, what you need is some wild, swinging from the chandelier sex, complete with three or four bone-melting orgasms—the perfect cure for insomnia.*

Trinity had learned quickly to expect anything from the youngest Adler, but seeing the towel he'd started to wrap around her slender shoulders fall away as she launched herself into his arms completely threw him for a loop. As much as he loved having the naked imp plastered against him like a second skin, the gut-wrenching sobs that followed were breaking his heart. Pulling another dry bath sheet from the warmer, Trinity wrapped it securely around Paris' petite frame before moving into the house, his long legs eating up the distance to the master bath in no time.

"I'm sleeping in the guest room down the hall." He already knew the defiant little wench hadn't used the room she was supposed to, but he wasn't going to share that tidbit.

"Didn't Evan tell you to use the master bedroom?" Trinity knew dammed well his cousin made it crystal clear which room to use before instructing his security team to monitor the outside of the room but to forward the inside feed to Trinity. Trin had quickly phoned Evan's people the first night to make sure they switched the feed; there was no way he was letting the guys in the control booth ogle what he considered his.

He felt her warm breath on the side of his neck when she sighed softly in acknowledgment she'd defied her new brother-in-law's instruction. Oh yeah, she knew she'd just given him another reason to bring the flat of his hand down on her perfect ass. Trinity had no idea *how* he was going to do it, but he was going to convince Paris Adler she belonged to him.

Showing her they belonged together was beginning to look like it would be a hell of a challenge since Paris battled her attraction to him like it was her damned job. Tonight, was the first time she'd let him see her vulnerability, but he wasn't foolish enough to believe it would last—and he didn't want it to. Her pain was piercing his heart. *Bring back the feisty woman who went up in flames over my knees a week ago.*

Before setting her on her feet, Trinity turned on the shower in the master suite's opulent ensuite bath, quickly adjusting the temperature and pressure. He made a mental note to teach her how to run the damned thing before he left. Trinity had helped Evan install the high-tech spa, laughing when the brilliant surgeon called him every day for a week, asking how to turn on his own shower. Setting her down beside the rock and marble enclosure, Trinity was careful to keep his hands on her until he thought she was steady on her feet. Quickly setting out everything they needed before checking the water temperature one last time, he turned to find Paris sliding down the glass wall.

"What the hell?" Scooping her up, Trinity settled her on the smooth marble bench inside the shower. He didn't claim to know everything about women but knew they always insisted on showering after swimming—something about how the chlorine screwed up their hair and skin. As a teen, Trin had spent far too much time hanging around the pool and for reasons he probably shouldn't mention, knew the women's dressing room had a variety of hair and skin products the men's locker lacked.

Toeing off his boots and tucking his socks inside, Trinity kept an eye on the quickly fading sprite staring blankly at the rock and plant-covered waterfall in front of her. He could feel her coming apart and hated knowing he'd pushed her to this point. Even more, he hated knowing he wasn't going to be able to resist if she gave voice to the need he sensed pulsing through her. Unbuttoning his shirt and tossing it aside before slipping out of his jeans, Trinity knelt in front of her. Tipping her face up to his with a touch so gentle, he saw her eyes widen in surprise, Trinity locked his gaze on hers before speaking.

"Are you sure, baby? Be very sure, Paris, because if I get in the shower with you, we both know where it's going to end, and that means you'll belong to me." He wasn't going to take what he knew she was going to offer unless she understood how it would change things between them.

Every shifter was blessed with unique gifts, and one of his was the ability to understand another person's motivations and needs. Trinity had always been able to sense the truth buried within someone—often before they knew it themselves. Any attempt to lie to him was futile—not only could he feel their authenticity, he could also smell the change in the person's physiological makeup when they lied.

"Please. I want you."

Paris' whispered words went straight to his heart, then promptly detoured to his rapidly inflating cock. Damn, she was going to make him lose his mind. Standing, he pulled a condom from his pocket and laid it on top of the shower's glass wall. Trinity leaned down to lift the petite beauty into his arms. *Fuck me, she is so small.* He needed to remember to go slow but wasn't sure he had that much control.

"Come on, Sprite, let's get the pool water out of your pretty hair first, then I'm going to enjoy washing it from every inch of your hot little body." He bit back a smile when she sputtered after he set her on her feet under the overhead showerhead. Moving behind her, Trinity squirted shampoo into his palm before pulling her out from under the spray. Washing her long locks, Trinity used his strong fingers to massage her scalp, smiling at her soft sighs and deep groans. Using the handheld sprayer to rinse her hair before adding conditioner to the long strands. The color of her hair reminded him of the waving fields of summer wheat he'd seen once years ago while driving across the country.

"This sprayer is a very handy device." He used it to rinse her hair again after conditioning it, knowing she had no idea how else he planned to utilize the pulsing spray. Taking his time, Trinity relished rinsing the long tresses he couldn't wait to see spread over his thighs. "Let's see how sensitive your pretty nipples are, baby." Wrapping one arm around her torso lifting her breasts, so the nipples were presented as the gift he knew they'd be, Trinity used one hand to pinch the first tip into a tight peak before focusing the spray on the tender bud. Paris gasped, pressing back deeper into his embrace. He felt her knees tremble, threatening to fold out from under her and chuckled as he moved the spray nozzle back to the wall.

Everything about Paris Adler called to him. His determination to make her his own had kept him from playing with another woman for the past year. Other Doms at Club Isola had teased him when he'd made the long trip to D.C. then left without participating in a single scene.

"You're so responsive. Damn, I want you." Sliding his fingers through her slick folds before lifting his hand to hold the syrupy fingers close to his face, Trinity let her unique fragrance move through him. Inhaling her scent, he felt his cock flex against her lower back. The difference in their heights was significant—hell, Trin would have to be creative to have sex with her standing up, but he didn't doubt for a second it would be worth the effort.

"Damn... why did you stop? Please don't stop. Your fingers were creating magic, and I haven't..." The airy quality of Paris' quiet words was the hottest thing he'd ever heard—until she cut them off abruptly. Stiffening against him, he knew she was planning to pull away, but he wouldn't let her unless she used a safe word.

Safeword. Fuck. They'd never finished their discussion of the basics. Paris Adler was going to make him lose his fucking mind.

Chapter Two

*F*UCK-A-DILLY CIRCUS. PARIS couldn't believe she'd almost confessed how long it had been since she'd had sex. When she'd seen something on social media about born-again virgins, it seemed funny at the time, but now she was worried there might be some thread of truth to it. What if her pussy was past its prime? Fricking frackers, she probably should have paid more attention during that damned Human Sexuality class she'd been forced to take her freshman year.

Why, oh why, hadn't she asked one of her sisters about this? Or one of her college friends? Fudgesicles, maybe if she'd dated more than once or twice a semester, she might have found out herself. Sighing, she reluctantly admitted she'd been too hung up this past year on Sheriff Stone to even look at another man. Ever since she'd met the bossiest man on the planet, the idea of any other man touching her sent ice racing through her veins.

"What was that thought, Paris?" Trinity's fingers tightened on her tender nipples, making her yelp. "Answer me right now. Don't edit, just tell the truth." Confess she hadn't had sex since the night she turned eighteen? *No thanks... I'll pass.*

"I was just worrying whether or not you are going to

fit because… well, you're pretty big." *Pretty big? Good grief, I sound like a dork.* By the time her brain registered his movement, Paris heard the sharp crack of a slap a split second before the cheek of her ass felt like it was on fire. "*Fuck!* That hurt. What the hell was that for?"

"Try again, baby. And let me remind you, you aren't the only one with special skills." His voice had dropped so low, the words sounded like they were being growled rather than spoken. *Special skills? Shit.* Could he read her mind? Paris knew Israel could hear Charlotte's internal dialogue, and Austin was finally able to tune in to most of it as well. Damn, she felt sorry for her sweet sister-in-law; Charlotte was never going to have any peace. Another sharp crack and the other side of her ass felt like it was on fire as well.

"Fucking hellfire with no redemption. Knock that shit off." When she turned to look up at him, the first thought to race through her mind was how much he looked like one of those cartoon characters whose head spins around on their shoulders as steam billows from their ears. Holy Hannah, he looked a heartbeat away from apocalyptic.

"Last chance, Paris. What were you thinking about, causing wave after wave of regret to pulse from your core?" Shit, he might not be reading her thoughts, but he was definitely tuned in to her emotions, and those were harder for her to control. "Do you know what a safe word is, Paris?" *Oh damn.*

"Yes, but I don't need it… at least, not now. I was just thinking I probably should have gone out more in college. I haven't had a lot of sexual experience." Pulling in a deep breath, Paris pushed her shoulders back, refusing to show how insecure she felt about the disparity in their backgrounds. When Trinity didn't respond, she wondered what he was waiting for. With five older brothers with varying degrees of dominant personalities, Paris was well-versed in their use of silence as an intimidation technique. *Give it up, Copper—been there, done that.*

"Did you just call me, Copper?" Holy hell, she'd said that out loud? *Damn, Paris, you really have to get out more.*

"It's that intimidate with silence bullshit. You're going to have to step up your game if that's the best you've got. I learned to ignore that nonsense when I was in the third grade." Shaking her head, Paris wondered how they'd gotten so far off track. Damn it all to hell, at this rate, she was never going to get laid again. "As the youngest of ten, I was subjected to all the usual intimidation methods siblings use. At this point, my immunity is probably off the fucking chart."

Trinity didn't respond for long seconds, making her wonder what was moving through his mind. She hadn't spent much time with him one-on-one, but it was easy to see he was no one's fool. She recognized his use of silence as a power play, but this was something entirely different... this time she swore he was listening to every emotion spinning wildly through her mind. When she finally took a calming breath, she realized his hands were tracing soothing caresses from her hips up over her ribs, his thumbs brushing the undersides of her breasts before his calloused palms moved back down to her hips. The move was an addictive combination of soothing and sensual.

"When was the last time you had sex, Paris?"

Damn... the one question she'd hoped he would be tactful enough to refrain from asking. Now her quandary was... should she confess or lie?

TRINITY WATCHED THE play of emotions on Paris' face and wondered which of the angels on her shoulders was going to win the age-old good vs evil argument. She wanted to lie, but he was certain she would opt for the truth in the end. Paris was too honest in her reactions for her to be deceitful about anything of significance. And he knew the question he'd asked her was definitely significant; her response had given her away. He let her agonize over the question for the better part of a full minute before finally moving his hands from beneath her ample breasts, pausing to bracket his calloused palms on either side of her face.

"It's a simple question, Paris. You're making this far more difficult than it needs to be." He suspected she was more intimidated by him than she was willing to admit, but that was a discussion for another time. While he was unquestionably more sexually experienced than he knew her to be, he was also far older. The gap between their ages was even more substantial than she knew since shifters ordinarily live much longer than non-shifters. His family was what was commonly referred to as *old blood*, whereas hers was *new blood*. His pack and family had been around for centuries, their lifespans far beyond the norm.

"It's a simple question with an embarrassing answer." Paris screwed her face up into the most adorable scowl he'd ever seen. "Does it matter? I mean, it's not like it's something anyone forgets how to do. I hear it's like riding a bike—it doesn't matter how long it's been, you can jump on and ride without any problem at all."

When he quirked his brow at her, Trin nearly laughed out loud at the bright red flush racing over her cheeks when the unintentional innuendo dawned on her. Hell, as blonde as her hair was, he could see her blush all the way to its roots.

"You know what I meant. I just don't see why it's important."

"You stopped yourself before you spilled the beans earlier, and your responses since then have only served to make me more curious. I agree with you that, in theory, it wouldn't ordinarily matter when either partner was last sexually active, but it seems to be important in this case. I'm not worried about you forgetting the mechanics of sex, Sprite—I'm more than capable of coaching you through it—but I am very concerned about hurting you." Using his thumbs, Trinity stroked the bruised skin below her eyes. Damn, they needed to get this resolved so she could sleep. If Paris was struggling with what happened in California, he doubted she was getting enough rest. Her overreaction to answering his question was another sign she wasn't functioning at her peak.

"I'm not a small man, Sprite. And you're a tiny woman. Under the best circumstances, I'd stretch you. If you haven't had sex in a while, I'll need to be particularly careful, and as badly as I want you, it would be easy to lose control. Shoving myself deep if you haven't been properly prepared would be damned painful and could potentially do permanent damage. Torn vaginal tissues aren't anything to scoff at and certainly not anything I want you to experience, Paris."

"Not since the night I turned eighteen."

She'd blurted the words out so quickly, Trin blinked twice before his brain processed the information. He could feel the humiliation pulsing through her, so he carefully schooled his features. Before he gathered his thoughts enough to respond, the little imp's entire body language shifted—it was the damnedest thing he'd ever seen. Hell, she seemed to have pulled energy into herself from thin air. Stiffening her spine and pulling her shoulders back, the air around her crackled as she gathered her wits about her.

"I understand. You've changed your mind. You are right, you're a big man, and I appreciate the fact you don't want to risk hurting me. How very gallant. After all, how would it look to have the Sheriff injure a woman with his ginormous cock?"

He didn't interrupt her speech, better to let her dig herself all the way to the rock-solid bottom before calling bullshit.

"Look, I'm tired. I haven't been sleeping all that great... you know how it is, a new place, a different bed, and all that. I think I'll just turn in now."

Does she really think I'm going to let her blow all that smoke up my ass, then simply allow her to turn her back on me? Maybe she isn't as attracted to me as I thought? Or she thinks I'm a fucking fool. No sooner had the thought run through his mind than he saw the first tear breach the lower lid of her bright blue eyes. Growling under his breath, Trinity grabbed the condom from atop the shower wall then scooped her up in his arms.

"That was quite the speech, Sprite. You missed your calling; you'd make a great speechwriter for some blowhard politician, but since you rocked your job interview a couple of days ago, I'd say any political aspirations will have to wait." She stared up at him, her mouth gaping open. Tossing her onto the bed, he crawled over her before she could scramble away. In five seconds flat, he'd shackled both wrists in his large hand and anchored them over her head.

When she started to speak, he cut off any potential protest by sealing his lips over hers in a kiss that started off as seduction but moved quickly to demanding. Her body was stiff beneath him, but he knew it wouldn't last. A desperate need, unlike any he'd ever felt from a woman, radiated from the deepest part of her core—she wanted him as much as he wanted her. Nipping her bottom lip, Trinity took full advantage of her gasp to push his tongue into her mouth. Exploring every recess of her sweet mouth was fogging his brain and stretching his control to the breaking point. Rocking his throbbing erection against her, he felt her shudder and the scent of her cream filled the air around him.

"Fucking hell, I want you until my brain is starting to melt." Any notion Paris had about him rejecting her could be negated by the heated, steel length of his cock pressing against her. Lifting until he could look into her eyes, Trinity tried to gauge whether to continue what was rapidly becoming a slippery slope or pull back, settle Paris in his arms, and let her sleep. When her eyes glazed over and her long lashes fluttered closer and closer to the dark circles under her eyes, he pressed a soft kiss to her forehead and smiled. *Guess she answered the question for me.*

Sleep well, Sprite, because I've got some wicked ideas about how to rouse you in a couple of hours.

Chapter Three

C LEVELAND ADLER LEANED back in the seat, watching the gauges spike each time his booted foot brushed against the accelerator of the most technologically advanced race car he'd ever tested. Hell, he was usually over-the-top excited about any new gadget, and this car was loaded with them. Ordinarily, Cleveland would have spent weeks studying the operating manuals rather than the cursory glance he'd given them last night. Leaning his head back against the seat, he wondered when he'd lost the passion he'd once felt for racing.

He'd always imagined retiring from racing after he'd socked away enough money to create his own team. After the wild events during his sister, London's wedding, Cleveland had started questioning his long-range plan. Maybe it was time to change directions. Sitting under the stars on the beach after the rest of the family finally drifted off to bed, Cleveland had stared at the rolling surf as his brother, Israel, did the same. They'd talked about everything and nothing before finally getting around to discussing business.

Israel's security business was growing faster than he could hire people he trusted, and without the unique skills of a shifter, anyone he hired was already working at a distinct disadvantage as far as Israel was concerned. The longer they talked, the more the seed of change had taken root. Cleveland had invested heavily in his brother, Bronx's car dealerships but had no interest in selling cars. Hell, at this point, he was having trouble being interested in driving.

A disembodied voice speaking in his ear pulled him back to the moment. Shaking his head, Cleveland cursed under his breath… damn it, he knew better than to become distracted on the track—that's how accidents happen. Slip-ups, especially when you're traveling two hundred miles per hour, are often deadly. Making a mental note to call Bronx, Cleveland hoped his brother had changed his mind about further expanding his string of car dealerships. It didn't matter how often Cleveland told his brother he had no interest in stalking customers in a car lot, Bronx never seemed to hear him.

Bronx Adler had spent his entire adult life building a business around his brother's racing success—using Cleveland's picture as well as his money. If Bronx had applied his killer business skills at Adler Oil, the company would have gone public years ago. Before leaving for the track, Cleveland sent out a text to all his siblings, letting them know where he'd be racing that weekend. He'd started the group texts after London attended a race with him several months earlier.

As much as the Adler brothers and sisters traveled, he never knew when one of them might be close, and the older he got, the more he enjoyed their company. If you'd told him ten years ago, he would intentionally spend time with his siblings, he'd have assumed you'd lost your mind... *Go figure.*

Hitting the accelerator, Cleveland pushed all thoughts of his family and their various businesses out of his mind as the car rocketed away from the starting line.

ASIA STARED OUT the window, the full moon calling to her. She hadn't run for weeks, and her agitation was growing by the minute. She'd shifted for the first time shortly after her thirteenth birthday and remembered how terrifying that first night had been. She'd walked out the back door of her family home, unsure what was happening to her out-of-control body. Stepping onto the slate patio into the moonlight, she'd begun changing in ways she'd never imagined possible. Panic seized her chest, making it almost impossible for her to breathe. Thank Goddess, her older brother had heard her through a telepathic link she hadn't known existed and doubled back from his own run.

Sighing, the woman the world knew as Adler Oil's legal eagle, wished she could leave the bed she was sharing with Franklin Cordesi without him knowing she was gone, but the man was a sexual Dominant to the core... he would know the moment her feet hit the floor.

"Cara, go for a walk in the moonlight if it will help you sleep. I would join you, but I suspect I'll sleep quite soundly as soon as the bed stops bouncing with your heavy sighs. I have an important conference call in a few hours, and I'd prefer to conduct it well rested." It was impossible to miss the unspoken message—you're keeping me awake, and I'd appreciate it if you would walk it off so I can get some damned sleep. Laughing to herself, she sent up a silent prayer of thanks to the Great Goddess for the save. Leaning over, she kissed his cheek before rolling to the edge of the enormous bed.

"I'd prefer you didn't go as you are. I tend to be a bit possessive with what I consider mine."

She paused, turning to look back at him over her shoulder, wondering why he was suddenly concerned with her nudity. After all, he'd rarely allowed her to wear anything since her family left the island. Giving her wrist a quick yank, Franklin pulled her back until she was sprawled over his chest.

"Make no mistake, Cara, you are *mine*."

It wasn't the first time he'd referred to her as his, but there was something different this time. Asia wasn't sure what had changed, but with her wolf pushing to run, she didn't have time to worry about it.

FRANKLIN WAS GRATEFUL he'd been able to find a shadowed spot downwind to watch the most beautiful creature he'd ever seen run on the beach, graceful strides skirting along the water's edge. The moonlight highlighted the wolf's sun-streaked sable coat as Asia Adler raced from one end of the sandy shore to the other. He'd watched from the bedroom window as she slipped out the French doors of their villa and into the dense foliage of the landscaped gardens surrounding their small slice of paradise. Asia had disappeared into the thick shrubs, but it was her wolf that emerged seconds later. Franklin held the clothes he found discarded among the dense cover; it was going to be interesting to see how she reacted when she discovered she would have to reenter the villa naked.

He'd known her secret before they'd ever met, having done his homework when he was hired to recruit Asia's younger sister, London, for the group of pharmaceutical companies known as The Consortium. Franklin knew all the Adler siblings' secrets—things they didn't even know about each other—but had no plans to reveal the gifts they kept hidden. He was, however, going to enjoy letting the beautiful shifter making her way back to the villa know he was privy to her secret. He liked knowing what others did not. Information was always power.

Franklin smiled in the darkness when he heard her nearly silent cursing from the bushes a few feet away. He'd already turned on lights in the villa, so she knew it was going to be impossible to sneak in undetected. Franklin had been dreading the end of their extended vacation in a few days, and the awkward goodbyes at the airport when they took separate flights back to their respective homes. Now, he was filled with a lightness he couldn't fully explain. Perhaps, it was the prospect of taking down another roadblock standing between them, or maybe he was just looking forward to surprising the most fascinating woman he'd ever met.

Chapter Four

P ARIS FELT HERSELF floating in the foggy netherworld between sleep and fully awake. Every cell in her body felt electrified, but her brain wasn't functioning enough yet to know why. When she tried to turn, her hands wouldn't move from their position over her head. *What the hell? I never sleep like this.* A moment of panic rolled over her like a two-ton truck.

"Hold still, or you're going to hurt yourself, Sprite."

"Trinity?" She was coming awake but slower than she would have liked.

"You were expecting someone else, baby?" She heard him chuckle softly before he continued, this time, his voice much deeper, more serious. "Be careful how you answer that, Paris. Some shifters share their women—I'm not one of them."

Share? Oh, hell no. She didn't begrudge her sister, London, her polyamorous marriage, but Paris wasn't interested in having a committed relationship with two men. Crispy critters, she wasn't convinced she could deal with one man full-time, so two was out of the question.

"No, I wasn't expecting someone else, but I wasn't expecting to wake up to my body being on fire with need and my damned hands tied to the headboard, either."

"Careful with the snark, Sprite. This is your only warning; I will punish you for that sort of thing in the future. And I'd suggest you clean up your language—quickly if you enjoy being able the sit down comfortably." The large hands wrapped around her thighs squeezed enough to act as a warning she wasn't wise enough to heed.

"I wake up bound to the fucking bed, and I'm not supposed to be pissy? *Seriously?*" Paris was fighting a losing battle between what her body was demanding and what her head kept telling her she *should* want. Before her mind processed the movement, Trinity flipped Paris over to her stomach, his palm landing four sharp slaps covering her entire ass. "Fucking hell. Knock it off that hurts." Another five swats seared the tender crease where her ass cheeks met the top of her thighs.

Tears burned the backs of her eyes, but she refused to give in and let them fall. *Damn it all to dusty doorknobs, I'm not going to cry like an inexperienced schoolgirl, even if I am inexperienced... I'm not a schoolgirl by a little more than a month. Dagnabbit, see what he's done? Now I'm talking to myself.*

"No, actually, you're speaking aloud."

Trinity's frustrated voice came from over her left shoulder, and Paris groaned. When would she ever learn? He flipped her back over to her back, making her gasp as her tender backside slid over the cool, cotton sheets. She pressed her lips together to keep from snarling when she met his gaze.

"At the resort, you told me you'd heard about safe words, yet you didn't use one. Why do you think that is,

Sprite?" Shrugging, she looked away.

"Shrugging isn't good enough, Paris. When I ask you a question, I expect an immediate answer—a respectful and truthful answer." What Trinity didn't understand was she hadn't answered because she didn't know the answer.

"I wasn't trying to be evasive. I don't know why I didn't use a safe word. We haven't talked about it since, but I didn't like you hitting me, it hurt. It didn't just hurt my ass... ets." Paris looked at him warily, but he just chuckled at her lame attempt to cover the inappropriate language.

"What else didn't you like, Paris? Take your time, think about how your body felt. I don't want to hear what you think you should say. More than anything, I want you to be self-aware enough to listen to your body rather than your head. Great sex may start in your head, Sprite, but it also relies heavily on body awareness."

Paris closed her eyes in an attempt to focus on how the punishment felt rather than how embarrassed she'd been by the whole thing. It didn't matter how she tried to spin it, Paris knew her tears weren't about the physical pain.

"I hated knowing you were frustrated with me." She tried to avert her gaze, but he wasn't allowing her to hide. Moving further up her torso, Trinity's strong fingers gripped her chin, gently turning her face back, so she faced him once again.

"The heart of submission is the desire to please your Master, Sprite. It doesn't feel right because you are new to the lifestyle. You've spent years gaining your independence and see pleasing me as losing a part of that hard-earned individuality. What you haven't had a chance to learn yet is you're going to gain far more than you lose."

"I'm not sure I can live my life just to please another person. I've been last in so many ways my entire life, I was looking forward to putting myself first after graduation." Paris found herself tugging on the restraints around her wrists, feeling as though her ability to communicate was somehow hampered. *Without my hands waving in the air when I'm speaking, how will anyone know what I'm saying? I've always used my hands to talk.*

TRINITY COULD FEEL the frustration coming off Paris in slow, devastating waves. Like many other submissives, Paris was struggling between what she recognized as her body's need for his Dominance, and her erroneous belief submission would make her weak. Trinity understood her dilemma as much as any man could—hell, he couldn't imagine giving another person the kind of power he would exert in her life when she belonged to him. As if she'd read his mind, Paris looked into his eyes, and he could practically see the little imp pulling her resolve around her like a cloak.

"Would you let someone tie you to the bed, Trinity?" The question itself wasn't entirely unreasonable, but the attitude laced through it was another matter entirely.

"First, when we are in a scene—and make no mistake if you are bound for my pleasure, *it is* a scene—you will refer to me as Sir or Master. Second, in answer to your question, no, I wouldn't allow it. I'm a sexual Dominant to my core. I wouldn't find any pleasure in the experience because it's not who I am. The woman wouldn't enjoy herself either. You see, Sprite, the Dominant's enjoyment is contingent on the submissive finding his or her pleasure—it's as simple as that—your pleasure feeds mine."

"I don't understand."

Her simple admission was all it took to remind Trinity how vital his role was. If he was going to show her the joy and freedom she could find in submission, he needed to teach by example. As the youngest in such a large family, Paris would have no doubt learned many of her life lessons by trial and error. Watching pack members with several children had taught him the youngest children in a family were often left to their own devices. Whether parents were overwhelmed with their older kids' activities or simply too exhausted to do it all again, the result was the same—the youngest didn't always get the same level of parenting as the older kids.

"Do you trust me, Paris?" Much to his relief, she didn't hesitate to answer.

"Yes. I don't think you would ever intentionally hurt me… well, not beyond what I've already experienced."

He smiled at her reference to the spankings she'd gotten, and she was right, Paris had already experienced the worst of his punishments. There were many ways to challenge a submissive, and Trinity was convinced orgasm denial would better serve his needs with the little spitfire he knew was his mate.

"You're right, baby. You've already experienced my worst. I'm looking forward to showing you how enjoyable a sensual spanking can be." When she frowned, her disbelief easy to read, he didn't try to hold back his laughter. "I promise to show you—later. Your beautiful ass is too sore to enjoy the experience now." He saw her eyes dilate as she registered the truth of his comment. "Let go of your need for control—just for tonight. Let me show you how amazing it can be. Trust me to take you where you need to go, baby."

"Yes."

Her whispered assent was all he needed. Slipping back between her shapely thighs, Trin admired the deep-rose color of the swollen folds of her labia. Inhaling her scent, Trinity was forced to shift positions when his cock continued to respond to Paris' intoxicating fragrance.

"So smooth, I love this unobstructed view. Being able to see the pretty petals of your pussy flowering open for me, weeping the sweetest nectar in the world in anticipation of my cock has my control perilously close to snapping." Trinity used the tip of his tongue to circle her clit smiling when he heard the headboard rattle as she struggled against the restraints. A fresh wash of cream coated the sensitive folds when she realized she was still bound. "Baby, you are going to have a hard time convincing me you don't like bondage when your sex just sent me a honeyed treat I have no intention of wasting."

Flattening his tongue, Trinity licked from below her vaginal opening all the way to her clit without letting up. Paris screamed and convulsed under his hold.

"That's one. Go again, baby." Rolling his tongue, Trinity speared it deep into her opening before pulling back to nip her clit. Damn, seeing her sweet berry fully exposed was going to make him lose control and shift if he didn't get himself back on track. Hell, he could already feel his canines elongating, the urge to shift spiraling out of control.

"Please, Trinity… Sir, I need you. Please fuck me." Her use of the honorific and bold request snapped the last fine thread of control he'd been holding on to. Moving quickly into position, Trinity tore open the condom wrapper with practiced ease, rolling it on without any hesitation.

"We're going to go slow, Sprite. I don't want to hurt you." Pushing his tip against her heated opening, Trinity ground his teeth in what was quickly becoming a futile effort to hold back. "What are you going to say if you need me to slow down, Paris?"

"Yellow. I'll say yellow if I need you to go slower, but what I really need is a word for *faster*."

He'd have laughed if he hadn't worried any break in his concentration would send him balls deep into her hot little body before he was convinced she was ready for him. Rocking his hips forward before pulling back out, Trinity was making slow, incremental progress. Great Goddess, she was so damned tight.

"Goddess, save me from temptation. Damn, it's like being squeezed by a hot, wet, velvet-covered fist. Fucking hell." Burying his face against her neck, feeling her blood surging so close to the surface, Trinity suddenly under-stood how Austin Adler had been so overwhelmed and captivated with his mate, he had claimed sweet Charlotte without her prior consent. The incident had been a topic of discussion while they were in the Caribbean, and he'd heard several members of the pack discussing it after they'd returned home.

"More. Please. More. Oh, damn, I'm so close, but I

want to feel your length deep inside me when I come." Paris tried to rotate her hips, then tipped them incrementally in a futile attempt to change the angle. "I can't wait to feel the ridges of your cock slide over my tongue as you fuck my mouth."

Fucking hell, the little temptress couldn't possibly understand what she was doing. Pushing him like this wasn't wise. Hell, he was already skating on the edge of losing control. She was pushing buttons she had no idea short-circuited his brain. The way her vaginal muscles tried to pull him deeper was testing his resolve, unlike anything else he'd ever experienced.

Trinity shifted his weight from one arm to the other so he could slip a hand between them, but before he could roll her peaked nipples between his fingers, Paris seized the opportunity to push her hips up, impaling herself on his cock. The petite hellion screamed his name as she gushed around him, the vice-like feel of her pussy squeezing him was enough to shatter Trin's control, sending him hurtling over the edge into a tunnel of sparkling lights, right behind her.

Pinpoints of light raced in a blur behind his eyelids, and Trinity could have sworn the top of his head was in danger of blowing apart. The pleasure was so much more than he'd ever experienced with anyone else, Trinity felt as if the Universe had pulled the rug out from under him. Sagging on to his forearms—so he didn't collapse on top of the angel of temptation—Trin tried to regain control over his breathing and hoped his heart wouldn't beat right out of his chest.

"Holy hell, woman, if I weren't so totally shattered, I'd

give your tender ass the swats it deserves for pulling a stunt like that." He'd spoken the words against the side of Paris' neck because his oxygen-starved muscles still weren't trustworthy enough to lift up and look into her eyes.

He heard her soft sigh and whispered, "It felt so good it was worth it."

Okay, maybe she wouldn't get those swats after all.

Chapter Five

WHEN TRINITY THOUGHT his arms would hold him, he lifted up to look into her eyes, relieved to see she appeared as dazed as he was by what they'd shared. She blinked several times trying to bring his face into focus before the sexiest smile he'd ever seen lit up the world around him. No woman had ever affected him the way Paris did. Damn it, she was going to take him apart if he wasn't careful.

"We have a lot to discuss, sweetheart, but right now, I want you to rest." A wave of emotion he could only describe as a cross between dread and resignation hit him dead center in his chest, stealing his breath with its strength. She wouldn't believe words of reassurance, so he didn't bother. Pressing a quick kiss to the tip of her nose before rolling off the bed, Trinity quickly disposed of the shredded condom, unconcerned because he'd known it was an exercise in futility when he'd put it on. Most pack members didn't bother with them, knowing the thin latex barriers couldn't withstand the forceful sex that was the norm for male shifters.

Slipping back into the bed, Trinity pulled her slender back against his chest and wrapped her in his embrace.

"Sleep, baby. Let me chase the nightmares away. You're safe with me... always." Feeling the woman Trinity knew belonged to him relax in the cocoon of his body, letting go, sliding quickly into sleep because she trusted him to keep her safe made him feel ten feet tall. He'd waited his entire life to find her—countless decades spent wondering if she was ever going to show up. Having her naked, sated, and sleeping in his arms was a life-changing moment.

He'd already released her wrists but planned to restrain her again before he woke her up for another round of off-the-chart sex in a few hours. The next time he had his cock buried in her heat, Trinity would be asking questions. He suspected Paris Adler was going to be one of those precious submissives who would sing like a sweet bird to get the orgasm her body craved. Trinity could hardly wait to explore every inch of her luscious body—mapping every one of her hot spots was going to be a pleasure.

Dozing for a couple of hours would be enough to recharge him, then he planned to slip out of bed and go for a run. He wouldn't stay gone too long, he'd learned during their stay at the resort, Paris became restless quickly if he left the room. It was if she sensed his presence and drew comfort from his proximity. Moving his hand up to cup her breast, Trinity smiled to himself when he felt her nipple peak.

Rest, first, baby, then we're going to chat.

PARIS WOKE UP with a start, shivering when the room's cool air rushed over her sweat-slicked skin. Pulling the sheet up to cover her bare breasts, she waited for the residual effects of the nightmare to abate. Laying her hand on the bed beside her, she detected a hint of warmth, so she knew Trinity hadn't been gone long. Pushing her shaking fingers through her damp hair, Paris struggled to push the lingering images of the recurring nightmare from her mind. Waking up to find David straddling her while holding a knife had easily been one of the most terrifying moments of her entire life.

Stumbling from the bed, Paris grabbed the shirt Trinity had left on a nearby chair and stepped through the open French doors. The smooth stones of the small patio chilled the bottoms of her feet, making her hiss a nearly silent curse and wish she'd pulled on her shoes. The master bedroom faced the wooded area behind the clinic and was surprisingly close to the secured perimeter fence.

A shimmer of light high in the trees caught her eye, the distraction causing her to step off the edge of the patio and tumble into the soft grass. Behind her, Paris heard something ping off a window and felt her heart skip a beat. She remembered London telling her the entire compound had bulletproof glass windows, and the walls were resistant to any heat sensing devices. Basically, the place had been her older sister's safe haven while she'd been hiding from big pharma.

Once London's research findings were published, the companies pursuing her were forced to switch their focus to damage control. Sucking in a deep breath as the realization someone had just shot at her washed over Paris, her mind was screaming at her to run, but something kept her in place.

TRINITY WAS ALREADY on his way back to Paris when he heard the first shot. Letting out a low-pitched growl he knew would carry for miles on the wind, he hoped like hell he'd scared the shooter into running. It wasn't ideal—Trin would prefer bagging the bastard himself—but under the circumstances, this was his next best option. Hopefully, the distress call he'd put out would bring in enough reinforcements to capture whoever had been ballsy enough to trespass on Monroe Pack land.

Trinity continued sending telepathic messages to Paris to stay down, but since he hadn't claimed her yet, he had no way of knowing whether or not she could hear him. The bigger question might be whether or not she would heed the warning.

Sprinting back to where he'd left her sleeping peacefully, Trinity heard a motor roar to life to his left and sent a telepathic update to anyone nearby. Fucking hell, he should have never gone so far. He'd known how easily she became unsettled without him nearby.

Before he could ask, Trin heard Seth Keller's voice waft through his mind. *I'm opening the small slider in the fence closest to the house, Sheriff. You won't have to break pace.* Trinity sent back his thanks as he ran through the low, narrow entry. Eli added the five-foot-high opening a couple of years ago; it was perfect for shifters and had proved to be a valuable addition to the security of the facility since it wasn't large enough for any motorized vehicles—hell, most adult humans had to stoop to slip through.

Once he was inside the fence, it was a short distance to where he knew Paris was huddled. He couldn't wait until they'd were able to communicate telepathically, but for now, he'd been forced to rely on sending his command to stay down on the wind, hoping she'd respond. Rounding the corner of the house, Trinity heard Paris' ear-piercing scream as he leaped forward intent on protecting her from harm.

Changing into human form in mid-air, Trin landed on his feet, lifted Paris' trembling form into his arms, and ran inside the still open patio doors. The scent of fear surrounded her, but she'd wrapped her arms tightly around his neck as he moved her back into the bedroom. He appreciated that she knew he would keep her safe.

"I can't believe he found me. How did he know where I was? I didn't tell anyone, but my family I was coming here." Sitting down on the edge of the bed, Trin smiled down at her when he realized she was wearing his shirt. Trinity didn't need to ask Paris who she was talking about, but he wished he'd insisted they discuss David Lamb when he'd first arrived to find her swimming naked in the pool.

"How did you know I was in trouble? Were you running in the woods?" He recognized the tremor in her voice; he'd dealt with enough victims to know one of the ways they reclaimed their control was by asking questions, so he waited, knowing there were more coming, probably sooner rather than later.

"Were you the reason I didn't move? I wanted to run, but for some reason, I knew I wasn't supposed to. Did he get away? How did you get through the fence? Or were you just running around naked in the yard? Wouldn't people at the clinic be able to see you?" Chuckling, he shook his head as the rapid-fire inquisition took a sharp left turn.

"I was running outside the perimeter fence, but Evan had a small, hidden gate installed close to the house when his clinic became popular. It allowed him to run off the stress without having the security of his patients compromised by opening either of the larger entrances. The security staff opened it as I was approaching, so I could run through without waiting. Seth knew I was in a hurry to find you."

She surprised him by running her hand over his bare chest in a slow caress. Trin would ordinarily consider such a bold move topping from the bottom, but he recognized the move as an attempt to put the trauma behind her, using any means available. It wasn't the best coping mechanism, but it was a common one. Laying his hand over hers, stilling her progress, Trin shook his head.

"Talk to me, Paris. You need to tell me about the man stalking you. Let me get dressed, and we'll go down to the kitchen. I'm famished, you can talk while I eat." When Paris reached for the jeans she'd discarded earlier, Trinity wrapped his hand around her wrist and shook his head.

"No, baby. You are dressed perfectly the way you are."

"If you think you're going to always get away with dictating what I wear, let me assure you, it isn't going to happen. My brothers and sisters have tried that shit my entire life. I've had to fight for my independence, and I'm not giving it up."

Trinity didn't bother to argue; she'd learn the truth soon enough.

Once he claimed her, Paris would belong to him, in

every way. His claim didn't mean he intended to control every aspect of her life. Trin had never wanted a 24/7 slave. He'd seen friends and pack members' relationships splinter under the tremendous strain those arrangements inevitably brought into their lives.

"To be clear, I wasn't dictating what you could wear. The command was about what you could not wear." Zipping his jeans without bothering with the top button, Trinity used his hand to motion her toward the door. "It so happens I enjoy seeing you in my shirt, knowing you are bare underneath. It's fucking hot, knowing all I have to do is slide my palm up the back of your thigh to the curve of your bare ass, and with virtually no effort, I can slip my fingers between your smooth folds into heaven." When she stumbled, Trin struggled to keep his expression neutral as she lifted her face to his.

"You can't say things like that, it's indecent." Before he could respond, she stopped dead in her tracks. "Oh. My. Goddess. I sound like somebody's up-tight granny. How did this happen? I just graduated from college." She returned her gaze to him and bit her lip. "Don't tell my family I've already finished. They are going to have a hissy I'm skipping the ceremony." Trin raised a brow in question, and she shifted her gaze to the floor.

"I don't want to be anywhere near David. After we talk, you'll understand, but promise me you won't tell Austin or Asia I've already finished. The others won't go crazy, but those two seem to think they need to fill in for Mom and Dad. Maybe Charlotte will keep Austin busy enough, he won't have time to shadow me. And now that I think about it, I bet Asia is going to be distracted by Franklin Cordessi. Just between you and me, I think everyone is underestimating him. I'll bet you rock, marbles, or chalk, he's as well-connected as Brooklyn's, Luke." Trinity picked Paris up and gave her bare bottom a smack making her wrap her legs around his waist. Moving into the kitchen, he sat her on the cool marble counter, smiling when she hissed.

"Stop talking yourself over an edge you don't need to worry about. I assure you everyone cares more about your safety than any damned ceremony. We can celebrate your success without watching you walk across a stage. Your brothers and sisters would not put you in a compromising position just to hear Pomp and Circumstance." *And I wouldn't fucking allow it.* Looking deep into her eyes, Trinity read her easily and sighed. Hell, he knew instinctively she was going to try to run. Damn, he needed to claim her as soon as possible, or she was going to disappear, and he'd play hell tracking her down.

"Listen, Sprite, I know it's tempting to run, but despite how it appears, you really are safer here than anywhere else. We've already called in enough favors to move the fucking moon to circle Neptune. We'll find him, and when we do, he'll be held accountable for everything he's done." *Assuming I don't tear the bastard limb from limb first.* "Now, stay right here and start talking."

"Pushy man. Crispy critters, I feel like I've jumped from the frying pan into the fire."

This time Trinity didn't try to hold back his laughter. *Imp, you have no fucking idea.*

Chapter Six

D AVID LAMB ACCELERATED down the highway, laughing as the headlights faded behind him. Whatever the asshole following him was driving, it was no match for his Porsche. The black truck had fallen in behind him as soon as he roared out of the woods onto the highway. He'd taken several turns, each one leading nowhere in particular, and the four-by-four had managed to stay right on his ass. Once he was confident they were tracking him, David put the pedal to the floor and watched them disappear into the inky black night.

He hadn't expected the woods behind the Monroe Clinic to be monitored, but by the time he'd seen the first camera, he was already in place with Paris in his sights. Shaking his head, David wondered what the hell kind of menagerie Dr. Evan Monroe kept inside his fortress. Maybe it was his drug-fueled imagination, but it appeared Dr. Monroe had the biggest fucking dog David had ever seen.

The car he was driving like a rocket down the road was too recognizable and much too valuable to drive cross country, so he'd keep driving west for an hour or two before turning around. He'd left the smaller of his family's private jets at a secluded airstrip on the outskirts of a suburb. Phoning ahead, he gave the pilot time to file a flight plan back to California.

By the time he landed in San Francisco, his mother's Senate staff would already have altered his flight itinerary, making it look as though he'd overnighted in Denver, spending time with friends who would be happy to cover for him. Everyone would swear he'd gone to dinner with them before retiring for the evening, then continuing on to the coast to attend a fundraiser for his mother's campaign. Senator Nancy Lamb would be floating in an alcohol-infused fog by the time she made her grand entrance into the ballroom and wouldn't question whether or not he'd shown up. As far as the good Senator was concerned, the event was a command performance her only son wouldn't dream of skipping.

He'd only wanted to let Paris know she couldn't hide from him. As soon as London returned from her honey-moon, Paris would quickly tire of living under the Monroe's roof. From what he'd been able to learn about the brothers her sister had married, they were both driven and spent most of their time working. Both men were known to frequent kink clubs and apparently considered themselves sexual Dominants.

It seemed the secrets of the kink world were well pro-tected by an ironclad non-disclosure agreement—the small bits of information David had been able to get on Elijah and Dr. Evan Monroe had cost him a fucking fortune. *I need to get my hands on one of those contracts, hell, the thing obviously scares the shit out of people. Dear ole Nancy could use it and might finally be forced to admit I made a meaningful contribution.* Keeping her people quiet was the biggest reason the woman had amassed a goddamned fortune on a salary that was considered laughable, compared to most entry-level CEO positions.

Paris had managed to stay one step ahead of him until now. He'd missed her by minutes in St. Barth's. If she hadn't left early, he'd have caught her on the road as he'd planned. Rumor had it, her family had hired the local sheriff to act as her bodyguard in the Caribbean. After hearing Paris complain about the cop she insisted was a Neanderthal, David hadn't been surprised she'd ditched him to travel alone.

Chuckling to himself, he thought back over the years of their friendship and wondered how the hell she'd missed how obsessed he'd been with her. Hell, David had wanted to fuck her the day they met, but it had been clear she was skittish, so he made a concession, playing the friend card. What he hadn't known was how long he was going to be relegated to that platonic position.

He'd meant it when he'd said if he couldn't have her no one would. David smiled in the car's darkened interior. She'd be scared now, and the minute she ran, he'd be right behind her. The men he'd hired to watch Paris were being paid well, they weren't about to let her slip through their fingers. Shaking his head, David had been surprised to learn Luke Grayson wasn't the security expert everyone believed him to be. It had only taken David a couple of days to hack into the Grayson's system. Hell, it was no wonder government systems were consistently being compromised if all their contractors were as incompetent as Grayson.

"Who were you expecting to snare in your little trap?" Luke chuckled as he leaned back in his oversized leather office chair and grinned at the large screen filled with his Uncle Mitch's crystal-clear image. Mitch was one of the world's best computer information specialists, with a network of friends who were as talented as he was—hell, some of them were even more skilled. It had been Mitch Grayson who'd gotten Luke his first laptop when he was in junior high, then mentored him until they'd become colleagues.

"Considering my wife's former profession, I considered it a safety measure. Not to mention Catalina, London, and Israel all bring things to the table that could easily spill over on Brooklyn." Although his little submissive was still gracing various positions in the top ten on the most wanted lists of more countries than he cared to count, she hadn't made a retrieval since he'd pulled her off Emilio Mendoza's island almost a year ago.

"I have to admit, when I set up the decoy server, the last person I expected to catch in the net was a senator's son." Twirling a pencil between his fingers, Luke shook his head. "Paris has considered David Lamb her best friend since their freshman year, then all the sudden, she stopped talking about him. It was as if he'd ceased to exist."

Mitch tilted his head to the side, one of the man's few tells. He was thinking, but he was also listening to what Luke wasn't saying as well as what he was speaking aloud.

"I assume you are feeding him just enough information

to keep him on the string. Is he tapping everything or just any reference to Paris?"

Mitch's position with Alex and Zach Lamont's ShadowDance Club had given him a unique perspective when it came to human behavior, and as an experienced Dom, he was well versed in the way submissive's minds worked. The Lamont's foray into the murky world of contract special forces meant Mitch had access to networks most people could only dream of tapping.

"Paris has evidently been dealing with a stalker for almost a year—not that she has bothered to share this information with her family. I found numerous campus police reports and two more serious reports filed with the local authorities." Luke hadn't been thrilled with the discovery—for one thing, it put him in a terrible position with the beautiful woman he called his own. Telling Brooklyn her younger sister's secret sounded a lot like tattling, but not telling her would almost certainly backfire later.

"Let me guess, the incidents started out so minor, she didn't think it was serious and by the time everything escalated to the point of being dangerous, she was worried her brothers and sisters would be pissed she'd kept quiet, so she's dug herself in and is trying to handle it herself." *Fucking hell, I've seen this shit over and over with subs. I swear they all think they're invincible.*

Luke laughed out loud because his uncle's thoughts were so loud, it was if he'd spoken the words out loud. Mitch was a gifted empath, but Luke's gift was stronger in almost every way. He'd always snickered at how well he understood Adrian Monk's assessment that some skills were both a blessing and a curse.

Jesus, don't tell me you are still watching those old reruns of Monk?

"Damn straight. Monk makes me feel normal."

"He isn't an empath, so you're comparing apples to oranges." Mitch's teasing tone made Luke laugh out loud.

"He crawls inside people's heads—so close enough." Luke enjoyed their easy banter, but he'd called his uncle for advice, so it was time to get the conversation back on track. "So, what do you think? Should I call Austin? I know he's on his honeymoon, but I'm not sure this is something that should wait." Luke heard the distinctive ding of a computer alert and watched as his uncle turned, frowning at another screen.

"I sent a message to the Monroe's security team, inquiring about Paris when you called." Luke had propped his feet up on the desk, but they hit the stone floor with a resounding thud. Mitch rolled his eyes and shrugged before adding, "When you set up this call, I put out some feelers. You think loud, Luke. Since the report on Paris mentioned a couple of significant traffic violations, I didn't think Sheriff Stone was the best place to start."

"But as it turns out, he's exactly where you should have started." Brooklyn's voice sounded from behind Luke, and he almost groaned. Her presence explained the flash of recognition he'd seen in his uncle's eyes a few minutes earlier.

"Husband mine, we're going to have a long chat about why it's okay for you to keep secrets from me, but I'd be spending time over the spanking bench if things were reversed."

Luke recognized the disappointment in Brooklyn's voice. She felt he'd let her down by not sharing what he'd learned, and B, as she was called by family and friends, wasn't far off the mark. His only saving grace was he hadn't received confirmation until a few minutes ago. Holding out his hand, Luke hated seeing the split second of hesitance in Brooklyn's eyes before she stepped fully into the room, placing her small hand in his much larger one. His chest tightened with the knowledge he'd damaged the trust between them. Hell, they'd been friends long before they'd become lovers, and at the very least, Luke was guilty of treating his uncle with a greater degree of transparency than he'd handled the most important person in his life.

"I'm sorry, baby. I should have told you when I first suspected there was a problem, but I wanted confirmation before I worried you." Their low-key wedding had drained her—shockingly so for a woman who was known for her balls-to-the-wall work ethic.

If his suspicions were right, his tiny cat burglar was going to be resting a lot more than usual the next few months. The emotions coming from her were so mixed, Luke was having trouble sorting them out, but the tidal wave of nausea was eclipsing everything else.

Turning back to the screen, Luke saw understanding reflected in Mitch's eyes. Giving his uncle a sharp nod, he didn't bother speaking aloud. *Find David Lamb. I'll call Austin as soon as I get B settled.* Luke deliberately blocked Brooklyn from their telepathic link, knowing she was already worried enough. Before he could pick Brooklyn up, she took a quick step back.

"Somebody shot at Paris tonight. I don't have as strong a connection to her for some reason, so I didn't see it... but I could feel her fear. She's okay, but I think she'll run in some misguided belief she can keep those around her safe." *Which means she'll be all on her own. Goddess, I hate to think of her out there scared and alone. Oh, damn, I don't feel so good.*

Luke shook his head in frustration as Brooklyn swayed on her feet, wondering how long it would be before she figured out what was going on.

Carrying her in his arms out of his office, Luke heard Mitch's soft laughter before he noted the screen going dark. *Take good care of my future great-niece or nephew.*

IAN MCGREGOR LOOKED at the caller ID on his phone and smiled when he saw Mitch Grayson's name. They'd been friends and business partners for years but communicated almost exclusively via video conference call. A phone call usually meant the ShadowDance team had come up against some kind of pressing challenge or significant piece of information about something happening on the east coast. Since ShadowDance Mountain was nestled deep in the Colorado Rockies, they relied on him if something came up in his neck of the woods, as his midwestern friends referred to anything along the eastern seaboard.

"Mitch, to what do I owe this unexpected pleasure?" Ian didn't have to wait long for the answer, and he didn't like what he heard. His lovely wife and devoted submissive had been stalked for years by the son of a prominent politician, so he understood Mitch's unspoken concern.

Since Paris was the new sister-in-law of one of his club members, the love interest of another member, and younger sister of two other long-time members, Ian felt a particular responsibility to the young woman.

"Unfortunately, I've had some experience with the entitled sons of politicians. They aren't smart but are usually remarkably resourceful. And their damned resources are well-funded enough to be a pain in the ass."

"Which is a polite way of saying mommy and daddy would rather dole out money than deal with the monster their years of disinterest and apathy have created." Mitch knew Callie McGregor's story, and like everyone else who knew her, he was damned impressed. Callie had worked for a local tabloid when she'd been tasked with sneaking onto Ian's private island to gather information about Club Isola, Ian's ultra-exclusive kink club catering to Washington D.C.'s elite. Unfortunately for Callie, the entire island was wired for sight and sound—hell, it was one of the most secure places on the east coast.

"Brooklyn thinks Paris will run, in some misguided attempt to keep the people around her safe." Ian rolled his eyes—damned if this story didn't sound familiar. "I remembered the bracelets you made for Callie, Holly, and Abby—among others." Ian had made high tech pieces of jewelry, complete with tracking signals and a panic button that brought help from multiple sources. The one he'd made for his wife, the wife of his best friend, and his friend's sister started what became a very lucrative business. Later, he'd made them for all his friends' submissives and wives.

"Is there a way to get one of the bracelets for Paris?

"Who's watching her?" Ian could feel the surge of protectiveness moving through him. Women should be treasured, not stalked. Knowing Paris Adler has become a victim enrages him. "The last I heard Trinity Stone was the Sheriff there and rumor has it he and Ms. Adler have been dancing around each other for several months."

Ian was familiar with Evan Monroe's clinic, hell, the place was one of the most respected private medical facilities in the world—the level of care, the skill of the surgeon himself, and the over the top security attracted the rich and powerful like flies to honey. Unfortunately, the best security in the world could be compromised, and Ian was glad Mitch had called.

"Sheriff Stone was running in the nearby woods when someone took pot shots at Paris last night. She wasn't hurt, but her sister will be returning home soon, and everyone expects her to take off, in a misguided effort to keep her pregnant sister safe." Knowing the great lengths Callie had gone to for her own sister, unworthy and wretched as she was, Ian wasn't at all surprised to hear the Adlers expected her to run.

Holding out his hand to Callie when she appeared in the open door of his office, Ian smiled. He loved the whisper of sound her bare feet made padding across the wood floor as she moved gracefully to him.

"Let Trinity know I'll have a bracelet to him in twenty-four hours. Until then, I have full faith he can find enough ways to contain Ms. Adler." Callie settled on his lap, one arm wrapping around his neck, the heat of her bare breast quickly penetrating the cotton dress shirt he wore. With their children spending time in Texas with family friends,

Ian once again insisted his lovely sub be bared to him unless told otherwise.

After giving him two beautiful children, Callie's body had changed in subtle ways, and Ian couldn't be more pleased. Of all the gifts he'd given her over the years, the one Ian was the proudest of was confidence. He'd even added some of the things he'd learned to the club's training program for Doms. Seeing Callie blossom in his care brought him more joy than he'd ever thought possible.

After disconnecting the call, Ian leaned forward, licking a circle around Callie's nipple then blowing over the damp skin, smiling where the nip puckered into a sharp point. "I love the way your body responds to my touch."

"Your touch lights up even the smallest parts of me, Master." Damn, he loved this woman. Her voice was equal parts temptation and challenge, but there was no mistaking the desire in her sparkling blue eyes. He was thrilled to hear the confident tone of her sweet seduction; she'd been so unsure of herself when she first snuck onto his island. Oh, she'd put on a good front, but he'd seen through her bravado immediately.

"I'm going to meet the challenge I hear in your voice, *Carlin*." At five-foot-one inch, Callie was petite by any standard. He'd insisted she continue her self-defense training after they'd married and admired how physically fit she remained, no matter how busy she was—her stamina was going to serve her well when they moved to the playroom. "I'll meet you in the playroom in fifteen minutes, pet." When she started to stand, he tightened his hold and shook his head. "It's been a while since we played, I want to remind you there is no shame in using your safe word, baby."

"Thank you, Master, but I've been looking forward to this for a long time. I've missed being able to give myself to you." Soft fingers stroked the underside of his chin, her eyes never leaving his. "You own my heart, Ian. Our love is the foundation everything else is built upon. Make your calls, get a bracelet to Ms. Adler. I could feel her pain through you and Mitch, I know you won't be able to focus until you know the beautiful piece of your genius on its way to her. She likes tanzanite. Just so you know." Ian pulled her into a crushing hug before setting her on her feet.

"I'm looking forward to our scene more than you know, *Carlin*. Every day you fill a place in my soul I didn't even know was empty until you came into my life. Your trust is my most treasured possession, your love a gift from God above." Watching her walk from the room, Ian sent up a silent prayer of thanks for the pissant manager who'd sent her to his island. The son of a bitch had planned to expose Ian and the members of Club Isola. He'd sent an angel in a rowboat who'd claimed Ian's heart the moment his eyes locked with those of his clumsy intruder.

Chapter Seven

PARIS LOOKED DOWN at the diamond and tanzanite bracelet Trinity had fastened around her wrist after lunch. Sliding the jeweled ring around her arm, Paris was enthralled with the way the stones reflected the fading rays of the afternoon sun and studied the recessed button he'd referred to as a panic alarm. She'd been apprehensive about the whole idea, knowing instinctively it was little more than a lovely anchor.

After she and Trinity did a verbal dance around the outer edge of an argument, he'd finally phoned the bracelet's creator, Ian McGregor. It had taken her little more than a heartbeat to know she was wasting her breath. The infamous entrepreneur was focused and informative, but it was impossible to miss the posture, tone, and demeanor of a Dominant. Paris knew she should be grateful for the gift, hell, the stones alone were worth a fortune, but the whole mess with David seemed to be spiraling out of control.

"Damn, I recognize that skeptical expression. It's the *I know you are blowing smoke up my ass* look all subs get when a Dom is playing every PCBS card in the deck."

Paris watched as the woman who looked like a Native American Tinkerbell bounced into view. It was hard to tell through a monitor, but the woman appeared to be about the same size and age as Paris. She studied Paris for a split second before grinning.

"Holy hell, I know who you are. You're Paris Adler. Damn, girl, it's great to meet you. I've consulted with your brother, Austin, and sister, Asia a couple of times. They are both so proud of you. I'm Abby Garrett by the way, and the two men glaring in the background are my loving husbands... Logan Douglas and Kalen Black."

"Love, this is a little over the top—even for you. Barging into Master Ian's office won't bode well for you if he decides to call it in."

Paris listened to the man standing behind Abby, marveling at how everything aside from his voice seemed to fade into the background.

"You see that look, Callie? I see it on women's faces all the time. I swear his voice is pure magic. He should be required to register it as a weapon of mass manipulation." Abby's comment shook Paris from her trance, and she grinned as a woman she recognized as Callie McGregor stepped into view.

When Paris started reading erotic romance novels in college, she quickly recognized her brothers as Doms. It hadn't taken much research to discover the premier kink clubs in the country, and Callie McGregor's picture had caught her interest. News articles about Callie's treatment at the hands of a ruthless politician and his wife had been few and far between, but as Paris thought back over the few she'd read, there were some eerie similarities in their stories.

"It's nice to meet you both. Mrs. McGregor, I recently

saw pictures of the resort you helped design and now manage. I was really impressed with the few images I could find. I'd love to see it someday." When Callie's face lit up, Paris didn't miss the look of pride in Ian McGregor's eyes; the man was obviously besotted with his talented wife.

"Please call me Callie and thank you for your kind words. I hear we have a few unfortunate circumstances in common. I'm happy to hear you've gotten one of Ian's bracelets. Mine saved my hiney, and even though I hope you don't need it... the sense of security you'll gain is worth the small intrusion into your privacy."

"You two get stalked because you're hot, and I get tossed into a trunk because my brain cranks out energy nonsense like a spoiled two-year-old gobbling chocolate bars. The world is going to hell, I tell you."

Abby's teasing tone lightened the mood and Paris suddenly realized how much she missed having friends she could joke around with. Since the stalking began, she'd found herself more and more isolated, afraid to go out, worrying the stalker's behavior would escalate. Abby's expression softened as she leaned closer to the screen.

"Wear the bracelet, Paris. It might well save your life. Believe me, the most terrifying moment of my life was when I realized the kidnappers had taken my bracelet and earrings." Paris must have looked confused because the other man standing behind her stepped forward.

"When Abby's primary and secondary trackers went offline, we knew she was in trouble." Paris saw the man's large hand wrap around the back of his wife's neck, and the dark-haired beauty seemed to melt under his touch. "There was a protocol for activating the third tracker, a call that could only be made by her brother or Ian."

"Three tracking devices?" *Holy shit, what kind of projects does she work on?* Paris wondered for a brief moment if working with Abby Garret put Austin and Asia in danger.

"Your family is perfectly safe, Paris. The group responsible for Abby's kidnapping wanted her to work for them—much like your sister, London. Once her research became public, the danger to her became negligible."

Paris stared at Callie, wondering how the other woman had known what she was thinking. *Damn, I'm starting to think everybody has some sort of magic skill and I missed out.*

"Your gifts are waiting for you to uncover them." Callie's words made Paris smile as Ian pulled her onto his lap.

"I hope you'll heed Callie's and Abby's advice, Paris. I'll let Abby tell you about the third tracker when you meet. She was forced to reconcile her gratitude for being found before succumbing to exposure, with her ire at sporting a transmitter she didn't know was there. In the meantime, I want to remind you if you activate the panic alarm, we'll begin recording immediately, so feed us any information you can."

She understood what he was saying and the realization her life might depend on the link sent fear rocketing through her.

The call ended with Ian and Callie issuing her an open invitation to visit Club Isola as their guest, but Paris had been too lost in worry to do more than nod her thanks. Now, after having time to consider everything she'd learned about the bracelet's features, it seemed even more reasonable for her to leave. London would be home soon, and the last thing Paris wanted to do was endanger anyone—particularly not one of her siblings or her unborn niece or nephew.

"I am getting damned tired of David Lamb pulling my strings, making me dance to his tune like a fucking marionette. Because of him, I'm painting a target on everyone I care about." On one level, Paris recognized she was reeling even as she wished for the millionth time, she could turn back the clock... Damn, there were so many things she would do differently.

Stop looking backward, focus on the future. The simple words of wisdom wafted through her mind. Paris remembered hearing her mother repeating the simple mantra often when talking to her children, but they'd never meant much until this moment. Sighing, she stepped back from the window. Turning, she was surprised to see Trinity standing across the room behind her.

Looking at him made her heart ache with sadness. Damn this disaster all to hell and back, Trinity was going to be hard to walk away from. Plastering on a bright smile, she started to pass by where he stood, leaning against the most beautiful stone fireplace she'd ever seen, looking both delicious and dangerous.

"What would you like for dinner? I'm not really much of a cook, but I can grill steaks and nuke potatoes. I'm beginning to miss my fast food fixes. Maybe I'll drive into Boston tomorrow and get lunch." *Yes! That sounded perfect.* She'd almost slipped by when his hand cupped her elbow. The movement had been so quick, it was little more than a blur.

"What did I tell you about lying, Sprite?" If she hadn't been so close, she'd have missed the softly spoken words.

The accusation grated on her nerves, despite her knowing he was making a legitimate point.

"I'm not lying. The only junk food I've had since leaving St. Barth's was at the airport on the way home, and everyone knows airport food is made by aliens, so it doesn't count." He stared into her eyes, watching her with such intense focus, Paris found herself fighting an almost irresistible urge to drop her gaze to the floor. *Damn it all to chocolate-dipped donuts, this isn't a scene, keep your head in the game.* When Trinity kept his eyes locked on hers, Paris felt something inside her flip. *Hell, maybe he deserves to deal with David.*

"Better." Keeping his hand at her elbow, Trinity pushed away from the wall and escorted her into the kitchen.

Better? What's better? I'm not better, I'm a fucking train wreck. Damn, I have five brothers who are, down to the last one, pushy and cryptic. How did I not see this coming?

TRINITY WAS RELIEVED to see the feisty spirit back in Paris' eyes. When she'd turned from the window, the overwhelming look of sadness reflected in her expression felt like a punch straight to the gut. He should probably be grateful Paris hadn't come up with a plausible excuse for traveling into the city. While she might well miss the fast food, he knew most college students favored, she'd feel much better once she settled into the healthier habits the pack had adopted more than a century earlier.

His ambiguous remark sparked confusion, but he'd

take the puzzled look over her earlier bleak one any day of the week. Leading Paris into the kitchen, Trinity grinned when she started to fidget. She might have asked what he wanted for lunch, but he'd quickly discovered she was clueless when it came to cooking a real meal.

During one of her visits, Trinity had sat at the bar watching her struggle to make a salad. Of course, he hadn't left well enough alone, when she'd noted his amusement. He asked, "Why didn't anyone show you the proper way to chop vegetables, Beautiful?" But it had been her sister, London who'd answered. Moving from the stove to stand by her sister, had been a less than subtle reminder London had her younger sister's back, despite the gleam in her eyes, letting him know her move didn't indicate anger.

"Paris wasn't interested in cooking, there were already more people in the kitchen than were needed or appreciated." When Trinity hadn't responded, London laughed. "Little sister was usually curled up in a tree reading. She was the only kid I knew who wore out her library card." Since he already knew how often the family moved while the kids were growing up, visiting a library often enough to wear out a card was impressive.

Now, watching Paris shift from one foot to the other while staring into the open refrigerator, he remembered her commenting how uncomfortable she'd be once her sister returned home. Obviously, the youngest Adler was well accustomed to being told to bugger-off. What she didn't seem to know was Elijah and Evan had already returned and moved London into the Alpha's portion of the main house. Having spoken to Eli early this morning to confirm they planned to settle Paris into what the security staff called the clinic house, Trinity hoped she didn't give them too much trouble about the gift.

Paris didn't know her sister was already home, sleeping peacefully less than a mile away. The Monroe's arrived home late last night, and both London's husbands had been adamant she rest before visiting her sister. When London tried to argue, Eli had simply called the tunnel and left instructions his lovely wife was not to be allowed access to a cart. "That's not fair, you know I can't walk that far." Even the stamp of her small foot wasn't enough to counter the dark circles under her eyes.

"I am not limited by the parameters of *fair*, Princess. You and the child you are carrying are my priority. If you will stop and think about it, you'll see I'm right. You are already exhausted—you wouldn't enjoy the visit, and you'd worry your sister." Trinity had watched the scene play out on a large monitor in Evan's former home office, grateful when Evan hustled their tired mate off to bed.

Refocusing his attention on Paris, he debated how long he should allow her to worry before baling her out. "Trouble, Paris?" He saw her bite her lip before she turned to glare at him.

There she is, the spitfire who caught my attention. Damn, I've missed her.

Chapter Eight

D AVID LAMB STOOD next to his mother, smiling as photographers snapped their picture. It had been just the two of them since a climbing accident claimed his father a few days after David's high school graduation. The climbing expedition had been a gift from David's mother, and he'd always wondered if she hadn't set the whole thing up. Blinking to bring himself back to the moment, David continued smiling as the cameras whirled.

The message David received a few minutes ago enraged him, but he'd carefully schooled his expression. Learning his own mother had sent men to spy on Paris infuriated him. David knew too well the Gestapo techniques she and her minions could employ. She would have no regard for Paris' safety or reputation.

It wouldn't take Austin or Israel Adler long to figure out who was calling the shots. Hell, his mother's team had even gotten a court order to tap Paris' phone, citing her as a possible foreign entity attempting to infiltrate Senator Lamb's inner circle. It was nothing more than pure fiction. Nancy Lamb knew full well Paris wasn't trying to make her way into her inner circle. Hell, one of the things he admired most about Paris was her disdain for his mother.

David alerted the men he'd left in Massachusetts to watch Paris; if she decided to run, they were going to have another team to contend with. Fucking hell, the more people hanging around that damned small town, the more likely they were to be caught. *Fuck, I hope my smile doesn't look as phony as it feels.*

As soon as he realized Paris had run to her family, David had upped the security on his home computer network, watching his accounts for any sign of outside monitoring but hadn't seen anything suspicious yet. Christ, now he had to redouble his efforts because his damned mother was probably spying on him as well. If he couldn't get his mom to call off her dogs, David would have to find another way to stop Paris from going through with the charges she'd filed.

For just a moment, he considered pulling something out of his mother's own bag of tricks—it had always amazed him how anyone standing in Senator Lamb's way was quickly dispatched. She might be his mother, but David wasn't a fool—Nancy Lamb was one of the most ruthless people he'd ever known. They'd be having a serious discussion as soon as they were home. He knew better than to confront her in a public place; her security team would intervene, and the resulting scandal would derail whatever agenda she was pushing this week. Fuck, the woman always had an angle and usually a target—David needed to make sure the good Senator didn't paint a bull's eye on his back…

LEANING BACK AGAINST the headboard, Luke grinned. "You just keep looking, fucker. You're only going to see what I want you to see."

"Who are you talking to? Geez, don't you ever stop working?" Looking to where his new wife lay beside him, Luke gave her bare ass a stinging swat. "Hey, what the hell? You wake me up talking to an invisible bad guy on your laptop, and I get a swat? Like tying me to the fucking bed, isn't enough? Geez, you take the cake, you know that? Whatever possessed me to think marrying you was a good idea? Oh yeah, now I remember, it was the promise of wild monkey sex... when's that supposed to kick in? Because I have to tell you, this laptop in the bed nonsense isn't cutting it."

Luke stared at Brooklyn, shocked at what she'd just said. She'd always been a night owl and still liked to get up in the middle of the night to train. After years of working as a retrieval expert for insurers, his lovely cat burglar was having trouble adapting to a more sedate lifestyle. Hell, he couldn't even keep her in bed without tethering her.

"You're tied to the bed because it's the only way I can keep you from sneaking into the gym when you are supposed to be resting." Until he was convinced Emilio Mendoza's followers had finally let go of the criminal mastermind's vendetta, he was keeping her close to home. If one of them had to travel, they went together. Brooklyn had not only stolen a priceless amulet out from under Mendoza's nose, she'd also exposed his insanity.

Luke closed his laptop before setting it on the bedside table. He would explain what he'd been working on later. For now, Luke wanted his sassy wife focused on the pleasure he could bring her. Brooklyn hadn't been kidding when she said he'd promised her mind-blowing sex, and despite her snarky remark, he'd more than delivered. She stared at him with glacial blue eyes, challenge floating around her like a cloud.

Luke's empathic gift had always been well-developed, but since claiming Brooklyn as his own, he'd noticed his ability to connect with people was growing stronger. Her magic was so much more powerful than anyone realized— magnifying his own gifts in ways he hadn't anticipated. Even B discounted the significance of what the Universe had given her, but he knew she was secretly beginning to worry it might be more than she was ready to handle. *The Universe doesn't make mistakes, baby. If the Great Goddess thinks you're ready, you most certainly are.*

Pushing David Lamb and the cluster-fuck with Paris from his mind wasn't easy because the man's obsession with Brooklyn's youngest sister was growing at an alarming pace. Luke had set up multiple alerts on both the regular and dark internet for every member of the Adler family. When Paris' name popped up on the campus police dailies, he'd immediately started investigating, and regretted not telling Brooklyn about the trouble Paris was experiencing. Luke didn't feel B was intentionally holding a grudge, but he was also aware things weren't the same between them.

His little minx had learned to block him, frustrating Luke more than he was willing to admit. The only time she let down her guard was when she was utterly focused on a task or overwhelmed by pleasure. He'd set up an obstacle/training course for her on the rock face of the mountain he called home and loved listening as her mind spun like a whirling dervish when she scaled the rocky surface. Moving over B—as she'd always been known to family and friends—he pushed the stray tendrils of her hair from her face as he pushed her thighs apart with his knees.

"Wild monkey sex, huh? What do you call what we shared in the playroom yesterday? I could have sworn you were the one screaming loud enough to register on the Richter scale." Entering her in one smooth thrust, Luke smiled at her sharp gasp. Making a mental note to update her later on David Lamb, Luke focused all his attention on the woman tied to his bed.

It had taken him years to convince her to take a chance and elevate their relationship to a new level. They'd been friends since their freshman year of college and B had always worried sex would ruin their friendship. Perhaps she'd been right in the beginning, but Luke had been ready to take their relationship to a deeper level long before Brooklyn had, and the interminable wait had been pure torture.

Pulling his aching cock out until only the tip remained nestled in her heat, Luke rotated his hips, teasing her, then growled when she strained against the bond, trying to reach for him. Shackling her slender, bound wrists with one hand to keep her from bruising herself, Luke set a random pace, varying the depth, intensity, and speed of his thrusts, relishing the way her vaginal muscles contracted, pulling him deeper. He felt their souls lock together in a way they'd never connected before, and his control shattered.

Mine! You've always been mine, B.

PARIS WALKED INTO a small table as she was sneaking through the darkened house. Trinity watched the petite shadow belonging to the woman who claimed his heart hop on one foot, cursing like a drunken sailor. It might have been funny if his palm wasn't itching to paddle her bare ass. As a shifter, Trinity's night vision was exponentially better than a non-shifter, so he'd been able to see she was on a collision course with the low table, but warning her would have given him away, and he wasn't ready to alert her to his presence just yet.

Trinity had known when he told her he was taking a night shift to relieve one of his deputies, Paris would seize the opportunity to run. If there hadn't been two different teams watching the clinic compound, Trinity would have let the worst escape artist in the history of the world get a few miles down the road before he pulled her over and tossed her defiant little ass in jail.

Donning his uniform, Trinity had watched Paris' bright blue eyes repeatedly dart to the closet, and the security team confirmed she'd watched from the window until he'd driven through the gate. She'd promptly begun packing, stuffing everything she could into one small suitcase. He'd driven around the compound, reentering from the back, and barely made it back inside in time to see her sneaking down the stairs.

Trinity didn't care about the damned clothes and toiletries she'd packed. Hell, he didn't even give a rat's ass about the short dark wig he hadn't known she had before seeing the video of her stuffing it into the side pocket of her bag. It was the passport she'd checked before sliding into her purse that was concerning. *Fucking hell, if she slips through my fingers and gets out of the country, I might not ever see her again.*

The hardest part of following her through the house and into the garage was staying far enough behind. He always wondered how the hell non-shifters coped with not being able to see in the dark—it looked damned unhandy if you asked him.

"What the fucking hell?" Paris cursed softly when she pressed the button to open the garage door, and it remained firmly in place. One of the many security protocols he and the Monroe brothers put into place when Paris returned to "house sit" was to route the garage access through the control center, initiating a procedure that included calling Trinity. Pounding on the button, Trin could feel the frustration coming off her in waves. "This sucker better open or I'm going to drive through it." He doubted she would actually drive through the door, but with Paris, anything was possible. Shaking his head as she tried to manually lift the solid steel door, Trinity stepped out of the shadows.

PARIS SENSED ANOTHER presence and experienced a split second of blinding fear so intense, she leap-frogged fight and rocketed directly into flight mode. Sprinting to the door, she heard a man's voice cursing, then calling her name, but nothing fully registered except her need to escape. The walk-in door leading to the courtyard was almost within reach when strong hands grasped her upper arms. Paris' mind went blank, muscle memory kicking into high gear. Spinning out of his hold, she pushed her knee upward, but he turned too quickly for her to make contact. Before she could make another move, strong arms wrapped around her like steel bands.

"Paris, stop. Now! It's Trinity. You're safe, baby." Paris sucked in a breath, ready to scream when the man holding her pressed his lips to hers. Fear spiked, but in the back of her mind, a familiar scent calmed the storm raging through her enough for the cognitive part of her brain to kick back into gear.

"That's right, baby. It's Trinity, take a deep breath. Let your instincts take control. Push the distress aside and think. You're at Evan's, no one gets in or out of the secured perimeter without my prior approval." Trinity rubbed his hands in soothing circles over her back and wondered what the fuck she'd experienced to cause such a mind-melting reaction. When she started to shake, he knew she was moments from the mother of all adrenaline crashes.

"Listen to my voice, Paris. Let go of everything but the words. You're safe with me, sweetheart. Let's get you back inside, alright?" Trin knew he needed to call Eli, so he'd know Paris was safe; no doubt Seth had already called the pack leader to let him know there'd been an incident in the garage. Looking down into her eyes, Trinity watched the glazed orbs roll back, grateful he already had her in his arms. Before he could open his mouth to speak, she collapsed against him.

"Seth, see if Evan's still awake." Trin knew the man

working in the control center would have been monitoring the situation and didn't doubt the younger man was already on the phone with Dr. Evan Monroe. "Ask him to review the infrared camera and advise." Trinity knew the adrenaline crash would pass, having her faint into his arms wasn't what alarmed him. The real concern had been her complete loss of awareness during her panic. Paris had obviously learned some defense moves, but she'd been too scattered to make any of them effective.

By the time Trinity returned to the living room with Paris cradled in his arms, her eyes were open, but her deer-in-the-headlights look made it clear she still wasn't cognizant enough to be left alone. He made a quick detour to the kitchen for a bottle of water before settling her on his lap. Since Trin hadn't received the call from Evan as expected, he suspected the good doctor was on his way. As he picked up his phone to call Seth, it signaled a new message.

In-coming. ETA five. Dr. E detoured to the clinic for meds.

Seth's message might have seemed abrupt to an outsider, but Trinity knew Seth had been trained since birth to protect the pack's secrets. A large part of his job was to keep careful watch over any pack communication utilizing public services, and since Trin didn't routinely carry one of the secure phones the Monroe brothers used, Seth had been forced to text. Trinity smiled when his phone showed another message, this one from the new Mrs. Monroe.

What did you do? Why is my sister trying to bolt? If you hurt her, baby and I are going to kick your ass as soon as I feel better. What the hell, maybe I'll just spend time with you. It would serve you right to be stuck with a sick, prego crab. I can't believe she was going to run away without saying goodbye. Damn, now I'm crying again. Tell my sister to stay put, or I'll go Nigel on her.

The woman in his arms was shaking, but when he looked down at Paris, he could see her laughing silently, obviously having read the message displayed on his phone.

"Who's Nigel?"

"Nigel Ratburn. Basically, she's telling me she is going to rat me out to our brothers and sisters."

"Nigel Ratburn? That name sounds vaguely familiar." Paris burst out laughing at his admission, making him even more concerned.

"He's the teacher in the *Arthur* books by Marc Brown. There are kids' books and a television show, but it was the early computer games I loved. It became a code between us, a way of threatening to tattle without our parents asking what had happened. By the time we came along, our mom and dad were so swamped, they were more interested in keeping up with our older brothers and sisters than navigating any bickering among the younger kids." Trin knew Paris hadn't heard Evan step into the living room—her lack of awareness of her surroundings was a significant concern.

"I'm worried about London, she told me she was trying to hide how sick she's been. I hope Eli and Evan are paying attention. Shoot, maybe I'll go Nigel on her grumpy ass."

"Not necessary, little sister." Since Trinity hadn't bothered to turn on any lights, Paris would only know Evan's voice had come from somewhere behind them. She screamed, launching off his lap before he could stop her. Tripping over the same low-profile table, she'd run into earlier. *Sweetheart, it would save you a lot of pain if you'd make a mental map of where all the damned furniture is.*

"Fucking kindling, I tell you. I'm going to turn that damned table into toothpicks and burn the whole pile in the driveway while I roast penis shaped marshmallows. Only a man would put a table in the middle of a pathway because they never have to hurry through the room with their arms full of groceries or laundry. That table is a menace to society. Evan is a doctor for Goddess' sake... wait, maybe it's a way to drum up business... or some sort of primitive alarm. You know... someone manages to get past all the high-tech shit, then this is the last line of defense."

Several things happened at the same time, and Trinity was left staring—wondering how he'd completely lost control of the situation. Seth's disembodied voice blared over the hidden speakers announcing Ian McGregor was on the line and wanted to be patched through. Before Trinity could give Seth permission to connect the call, Paris bent over in front of him to roll up her pant leg. The view of her rounded ass cheeks showcased in a pair of jeans so tight, they looked as though they'd been painted on sent a surge of blood to his cock. *Fucking great, just what I need right now, a hard-on from hell.* And Dr. Monroe burst out laughing so hard he was leaning against the damned wall.

"Look at this shit. I'm bleeding. There's a fucking gash in my leg. Fuck a waddler, I'll probably have to get a frick-fracking tetanus shot. I'd rather buy a ticket on the fucking Titanic than get a shot. Fuck a pink duck in rubber boots."

A bark of laughter over the speakers let Trinity know Ian McGregor's call was already connected, and he'd been listening in on Paris' mini-meltdown.

"Paris, you have no idea how happy I am to hear you are safe." Trinity shook his head in disbelief. Hell, he felt like he'd been dropped into the middle of some damned sitcom. What a complete cluster fuck.

"Safe? Hell no, I'm not safe. This place is a damned obstacle course." There was a stark difference between the little hellion's words and expression. Evidently, she'd surfaced enough from the second round of adrenaline to regain some focus. "Why... how... wait a minute... what made you think I wasn't safe?" Trinity watched her eyes clear as her brows drew together in concentration.

"Your heart rate and respiration spiked and stayed off the chart long enough to indicate a problem, so the control center at the club called me. I've been watching your monitor on my laptop. You've been all over the place, sweetness. What the hell is going on up there?" Trin could hear the thread of amusement in Ian's voice, but he doubted Paris would notice. "Trinity, do you need any extra manpower?" Paris rolled her eyes, but Trin saw the corners of her mouth twitch. "Or perhaps you'd like to bring Paris to Club Isola, I believe we have an empty apartment."

"I admit, having her captive on an island holds a certain appeal."

"My only concern is what sort of mischief Paris and Callie could find." Ian paused, and Trin would bet the man was grinning ear to ear. "We'll continue to monitor Ms. Adler's autonomic responses, but since it seems you have things under control... Well, except for the overly aggressive table. I'd suggest you move the offending piece of furniture before it hurts someone else." By this time, Evan was chuckling again, and Paris was blushing so deeply, Trinity could feel the heat from several feet away. "Evan, I'd suggest you have your maintenance staff lock up their saws—just as a precaution."

Trinity heard a phone disconnect before Seth was back on the line, trying valiantly to keep from laughing as he signed off as well.

Chapter Nine

E VAN WATCHED PARIS' meltdown with barely con-
strained amusement, grateful she'd found a safe way
to expend the adrenaline overload. His new sister-in-law
was hiding some dark secrets, and from the thunderous
look on Trinity's face, the man fully intended to uncover
them all. Evan had detoured through the clinic on the way
to check on a post-op patient and to pick up something to
settle Paris down, but it looked like she'd found a far more
entertaining way to work through the backwash of adrenaline. There was still a crash coming, but a toe-curling
orgasm and a few hours' sleep would be the best things for
her.

Studying Paris carefully, it was easy to see the youngest
of his extended family was fully aware she was in trouble
for trying to leave. The truth was, he understood better
than she knew. The desire to protect those you love is a
powerful motivator, and for a submissive, it was an almost
overwhelming need. Subs were the world's most selfless
peacekeepers—willingly sacrificing their time, money, and
often their safety to make sure everyone around them
remained happy.

One of the things Evan always admired about Ian

McGregor was his dedication to protecting the submissives at Club Isola. He intervened to advocate for them when he knew they would never speak up for themselves. Ian had told him once, no matter how poor a man was, he could always give his partner the most valuable gift in the world—the confidence to use their own voice. It was a lesson Evan had never forgotten.

Evan and his brother pledged to rebuild their bride's confidence, which had been shaken to the core by the events leading up to her releasing the research that had put her dead center on the radar of a dangerous group of pharmaceutical companies known as The Consortium. The ever-evolving group had also targeted Joelle Morgan, so their wide circle of friends had been well-prepared to advise them about protecting London. Brandt and Ryan Morgan, Joelle's husbands, had teased Evan and Eli that they'd soon learn all the challenges of marrying a brilliant chemist.

Looking at Paris, he couldn't help but wonder what challenges Trinity would face, trying to contain her fiery spirit without suppressing it. Trin was fighting to keep his frustration from steamrolling the little hellion, a struggle Paris sensed, judging by the way she was fidgeting. Paris was enough like London, Evan could practically predict the moment she was going to flip from defense to offense.

3… 2… 1…

"I don't know why you're so angry. I was doing you all a favor. If I leave, you won't have to deal with David and his mother, and let me tell you, dealing with Nancy Lamb is not for the faint of heart. She will probably live forever because Satan and all the minions in hell are afraid of her."

And there it was. The posture shift to defiance. Evan

laughed to himself because he'd seen it with each of the Adler siblings—the deeply ingrained *the best defense is a strong offense* mentality.

"It's not going to work, Paris. Don't play that card, it'll just piss me off." The low pitch of Trinity's voice had been known to scare pack kids into confessing everything from skipping school to criminal acts, but Paris simply pulled her shoulders back further and stared indignantly at the sheriff.

As much as Evan would like to stay and watch the fireworks, he wanted to return to his wife even more. After London had a chance to rest, they'd be having a long chat about concealing how ill she'd been. Damn, he thought they'd been watching their new wife carefully, but it seemed she was more resourceful than they'd realized.

Great Goddess, they were fools. Evan and Eli had both underestimated their mate, which itself was remarkable since she was one of the most respected vaccine research-ers in the world. *Damned stupid to forget how brilliant she is—a mistake we won't repeat.*

"I know Trinity is going to tell you many of the reasons you are safer here than out on your own, Paris, but until he's officially claimed you, I can still pull rank." Paris spun toward him, hands planted on her curvy hips, fire flaring in her eyes. She was all big glares and attitude—five foot three inches of defiance. *Yeah, Trin's life is going to be much more interesting now.*

"What do you mean, pull rank?" She cast a furtive look at Trin before returning her scowl to him. "Trinity isn't going to claim me. I'm a pain in his ass. Besides, I haven't heard back from the committee for your pack's school, so I've sent out a couple of resumes to schools in Texas. I always worried about living close to Austin, but I'm counting on Charlotte to keep him so busy he doesn't have time to micromanage me."

Evan watched as Trinity's entire body tensed. *Oh yeah, the good Sheriff is a split second away from going totally apocalyptic.*

"Eli will be calling to set up an appointment to discuss the terms of your employment, Paris. Word on the street is you owned the committee, sweetness. They haven't stopped singing your praises and were worried you would find another position if my brother and I didn't get our asses home—their words, not mine. Eli was adamant the committee wait until he was available to handle the contract's final details. He's a hell of a negotiator, be grateful he's advocating *for* you." The relief in her eyes made his heart clench.

Damn, Eli should have let the committee, or at least their dads, tell Paris how impressed they'd been with her passion for the special educational requirements of shifter children. She'd outlined the importance of teaching pack history as well as meeting their increased need for physical activity. She'd already developed a core curriculum that was better than any of the packages the group had reviewed. The members of the interview committee had been blown away by the recent graduate's level of understanding of the inherent challenges of starting a new school. The compensation package she was going to be offered would make the offer impossible to refuse, and once she was mated with Trinity, they hoped she'd teach several generations of shifters.

"Thank you... I mean thank you for telling me. I'm

looking forward to talking to Eli. If everything works out, I'll start looking for an apartment right away. If you have any recommendations, I'd appreciate the guidance."

"Accommodations will be a part of the salary package, sweetness," Evan smiled and shook his head. "We'd like for you to live here—in this house, I mean. It's a win-win for everyone." Evan wanted to smile at her surprised look. "London will love having you close; you'll be a huge help to her when the baby comes. Perhaps you can help us keep her from working herself into exhaustion."

"You're trying to tell me the two of you can't control your mate?" For the first time since he'd arrived, Paris gave him a genuine smile.

"We could, but I'd prefer she was speaking to me when our child is born."

"The struggle is real, new brother mine." Paris nodded her head in apparent understanding, then snickered. "I feel your pain."

Yeah, she might understand where he was coming from, but there wasn't a chance in hell she was offering any genuine sympathy. *Brat.* Evan watched her, relieved to see some of the tension drain from her slender form. Tipping his head in her direction, Evan addressed Trin,

"Make sure she gets some sleep. I'm heading back to my wife—we need to have a chat about withholding information. She's already racking up a long list of punishments for after the baby arrives." As a physician, Evan knew paddling his wife's luscious derriere wouldn't harm the child nestled safely inside her womb, but as a man looking forward to becoming a father for the first time, he wasn't willing to take any chances.

"London is going to play you like a song. She once delayed being grounded for two years. I assure you our parents would have forgotten if Asia hadn't come home from college and reminded them. Asia was ruthless about keeping track of those kinds of things. She has always been all about justice. I was convinced she'd become a big-time prosecutor."

Evan had seen her quick glance toward Trin at the mention of *justice*. Evan wanted to laugh out loud at the tension rippling through the room as his cousin stood stoic, arms crossed over his chest, watching Paris, just as the cat watches the canary.

Evan left the medication he'd bought for her in case she had trouble sleeping but doubted she'd need it. It was easy to see Paris was running on fumes. No doubt she'd deliberately wound herself up to stay awake until she was well out of Trinity's jurisdiction. She hadn't expected the garage doors to be locked and probably assumed she'd be able to drive out the front gate as she had when her sister Brooklyn had been a clinic patient. Smiling as he drove through the tunnel, he wondered what creative punishment Trin would come up with for Paris.

PARIS WATCHED THE door close behind Evan, realizing she was once again alone with Trinity. A shudder quaked from her core at the unnerving thought.

"Are you afraid of me, Paris?"

Trinity's question surprised and confused her. What had she done to make him think she was frightened? *Could have been the fight you put up within the garage, Paris. Good grief, nothing like completely losing it in front of the man who already has reservations about you.*

"I asked you a question, Sprite, and I expect an answer. You're already in enough trouble, there's no need to add to it." *So much for him giving me a free pass.*

"No, I'm not afraid of you… well, not in the way you're thinking." She watched from across the room as he tipped his head to the side, regarding her and could almost see him taking in every nuance of her reactions. The more she tried to control her physical responses, the more exaggerated they became. Black dots danced in her vision, making her wonder what would happen if they merged together.

"Breathe, baby." The command came from directly in front of her, and Paris wondered how he'd moved so quickly. She tried to pull in a deep breath, but it was as if someone had piled concrete blocks on her chest. The room spun rapidly to the right before somebody with a wicked sense of humor turned out the lights.

TRINITY BARELY CAUGHT Paris before she collapsed into a heap. By the time he realized she wasn't breathing and closed the gap between them, she was already going down. Her answer to his question hadn't surprised him, though he suspected she was mystified by the way her body responded to him. As he walked down the hall to the master bedroom, he felt her stir and knew she was already coming around.

"I can walk."

"I'm sure you can." If she thought she was going to call the shots, she was in for a big surprise. He'd let her run rampant earlier because he'd known it was a safe way for her to blow off the full head of steam her fear had created and burn the adrenaline coursing through her veins, but she'd drained all his patience, and now she would deal with the consequences. "Forgetting to breathe is not acceptable behavior for a sub, Paris. I would have thought in all your reading, you would have noted a pattern."

"Pattern?"

"Don't pretend like you don't understand—it's beneath you."

"Beneath me? What the hell? Put me down this minute, you big oaf. Boy, you take the cake, you know that. You lied about having to work. What would you say if I lied to you? Huh? What?"

"You did lie to me, Sprite. When I left, I told you I'd see you in the morning. Do you remember what you said?" *I swear if she lies, I'm not going to let her come for a fucking month.*

"I said, 'okay.' That's not a lie."

"Swear to the Goddess, you would test the patience of a saint—and baby, I'm no saint." Setting her on her feet, Trin took a step back, crossed his arms over his chest, and growled, "Strip." Her eyes widened as her mouth dropped open, but her pupils dilated, and he could see her pulse pounding at the base of her throat, so he knew she was aroused rather than frightened. "Strip, or I'll help you. And my assistance comes at a steep price." Nodding to her clothing, he added, "And your traveling clothes will be in

81

tatters when I'm done—though that plan does hold a certain appeal. Perhaps I should keep you naked until your job starts this fall?"

"You can't do that. I have meetings to attend."

"Your meeting is with a Dom, darlin.' Don't think for a minute your nudity would so much as make Eli Monroe blink." Sucking in a deep breath, Trinity savored the scent of her arousal. He reached for the buttons at the front of her shirt, but she shook her head and stepped back.

"Fine. Damn. You are so stinking pushy. Did anyone ever tell you that?"

"Not unless they were interested in paying for it. I'll be adding swats for that comment. I want you naked in ten seconds. Every second after that doubles the number of swats you've already earned, so I would stop wasting time if I were you." He made a point of looking at his watch as she scrambled to strip out of several layers of clothing. Hell, how had he missed the fact she was wearing so much. *What the fuck?* When she'd shed three shirts, two pair of leggings, a pair of jeans, and several pairs of panties—he intended to make disappear, Trin shook his head in disbelief.

"Why?" He waved his hand at the pile of discarded clothing, knowing he wouldn't have to explain further.

"I didn't know how much I'd need, and I hate checking bags at the airport. It... well, it slows you down."

"Slows you down or exposes you to more security cameras, making you easier to track?" Trinity was getting more pissed by the minute. If he didn't get this over with quickly, he was going to be too mad to punish her. He'd never put a submissive at risk by carrying out a punishment when he didn't have control over his emotions.

"Well... there is that, but in my defense, I wasn't running *from you*. I was running *to protect you*. You, London, and her husbands... and especially my niece or nephew."

Trinity watched her for several long seconds, before sighing. He knew Paris was telling the truth, and it frustrated him she hadn't shared those fears before trying to run. It wasn't enough to make him set aside her punishment, but it had calmed him enough, he was willing to reassess the scene he'd envisioned walking down the hall.

Instead of the more impersonal option of bending her over the edge of the bed, Trinity engulfed her small hand in his much larger one, leading her to the seating area in front of the massive stone fireplace. Within seconds, he had Paris draped over his lap, her pert ass positioned in a perfect peak. Caressing the rounded globes to bring the blood to the surface to minimize bruising, Trin smiled when she relaxed over his knees like a limp ragdoll.

"Your ass is spectacular, baby. It's a fucking work of art, and I'm looking forward to seeing my handprints layered one atop another. Take these swats with dignity, you earned them by not trusting me. The next time you think about running, remember the sting of consequences." A solid slap of his hand covered both cheeks, making her yelp in surprise. Before she could suck in a breath to sass him, he'd landed two more before stopping to admire the bright red outlines of his hands. Trinity was well aware of his own strength and would never give Paris more than she could endure, but the sudden tang of her arousal indicated her tolerance level was likely far beyond what either of them anticipated.

"You are mine, Paris. I'd give my life for yours without a second thought. Anyone intent on hurting you will have to go through me—and that won't be easy. Right now, there are two teams of men watching this facility—one with connections to Senator Lamb, the other seen talking to a man matching David Lamb's description." Paris jerked, arching her back so suddenly she would have rolled off his lap if he hadn't anticipated the move. Several more swats finally settled her down enough, he could once again smell her sweet honey.

Slipping his fingers into the gap at the top of her thighs, Trin let the calloused tips slide through her drenched folds. Using enough pressure to tease but not enough to push her closer to the release her body was begging for, Trin watched beads of sweat pop to the surface of her narrow back. His much darker hand was a sharp contrast to her pale ivory skin, making him wonder what color her fur would be when she shifted. Not all human mates made the change after mating, but Trin was convinced with Paris' family history, his spirited mate would make the change.

"I'm not sure this spanking has been the deterrent I'd hoped for—baby, you're drenched. Your needy little pussy is clenching around my fingers, trying to pull them deeper. One stroke over your G-spot would send you over the edge, wouldn't it, Sprite?" Her vaginal muscles were beginning to quiver, telling him she was seconds away from release. Pulling his finger from her, he smiled at her whispered curse.

"Do. Not. Come. Paris." Trin emphasized the command with a stinging swat before setting his spitting-mad future mate on her feet. The defiance glittering in her blue eyes was so easy to read, it was almost laughable. If he left her alone for thirty seconds, she would get herself off without thinking twice. "Kneel and thank your Master for the lesson." He should have known when he saw amusement flash in her expression, a split second before she masked it, the little hellion wasn't going to play it straight. Kneeling in near perfect form, she gave him the phoniest look of contrition Trinity had ever seen.

"Your humble servant thanks Master for the lesson. She understands now, he views her as too inept to take care of herself. She also appreciates the insight into how Doms use sex as a weapon. Sadly, the D/s lifestyle seems to have lost its appeal." Trinity was so stunned, he barely registered Paris rolling back onto her feet and stomping into the ensuite. By the time he recovered enough to move to the door, Paris had already closed it so quietly, the sound seemed to reverberate through the room. Before he could reach for the knob, he heard the distinctive click of the lock engaging.

What the ever-loving fuck? She isn't going to be able to sit for a week.

Chapter Ten

PARIS STARED INTO the beveled edged mirror, wondering who the stranger was looking back at her. The woman in the mirror was naked, flushed from arousal and anger, her hair in such disarray, she looked like some of her bulbs weren't screwed in all the way. Feeling the telltale burn at the back of her eyes, Paris watched tears streak down her flushed cheeks. Wiping them away with the back of her hand, she straightened her spine.

"I will not cry. Not getting a damned orgasm is not the end of the world. Get the hell out of here, then you play all you want. I should be able to find some guy willing to give me what I want." The pep talk she was giving herself wasn't working, so she gave up and moved to the shower. She'd get cleaned up, then try to rest. "Suck it up, Paris. You've got a safe place to sleep, plenty to eat, and the promise of a job you know is perfect for you. Be grateful and stop expecting tall, dark, and bossy to worship the ground you walk on."

By the time she'd finished her shower and dried her hair, Paris was ready to crash. She wrapped herself in the soft terry robe she found in a vanity drawer before opening the door. Stepping out of the bathroom, Paris wasn't surprised to see Trinity leaning against the fireplace mantel, ankles crossed in a deceptively casual pose. She might have misjudged his interest in her, but she wasn't without any people skills. He was wound tight. *Not my problem.*

"What are you doing, Sprite?"

"I'm exhausted. I'm going to sleep… alone. Go away." Paris could have sworn she heard him growl. He could blow that scary wolf routine up somebody else's ass, she didn't have the time or inclination to play his little mind games tonight. Turning out all the lights but the small lamp on the bedside table, Paris looked down at the robe before looking up at the man staring at her from across the room. Fucking hell, she wanted to change into something she'd be more comfortable sleeping in. Paris loved her sexy nightgowns, but she wasn't about to change in front of him. *Damn and double-damn.*

Crawling between the sheets wrapped in a thick robe wasn't easy, but she managed it without losing too much dignity. She hesitated when reaching for the small lamp. Since the night David broke into her apartment, she hadn't been able to sleep in the dark… until Trinity. Paris slept like a baby wrapped in his arms. Frack she dreaded having the nightmares return. *Don't let him know your weakness. You're an Adler and Adlers don't fold.*

Switching off the light, Paris settled into the bed and sighed. Closing her eyes, she tried to pretend tonight had never happened. Everything had been fine until she'd realized people were watching the compound. Trinity and his band of merry spies might not have considered her competent enough to share the information until an hour ago, but that didn't mean she hadn't sensed them. Damn, she hated being treated like a child. She'd dealt with this same bullshit her entire life and was over it. Despite her best efforts, she felt the first tear trickle silently from the corner of her eye.

TRINITY WATCHED PARIS hesitate to turn off the light, the anxiety pulsing around her was the only thing keeping him in place. The stunt she'd pulled before locking herself in the bathroom was over the top, but once he'd calmed down, Trin tried to put himself in her position. While they were in the Caribbean, he'd known she was skating on the edge—hell, it was the reason he'd started snooping. Now, he worried he'd tripped enough internet alerts to give her stalker a place to start looking after she vacated her California condo in the middle of the night.

Paris turned her back to where he was standing, but with his enhanced night vision, he could still see her clearly. When he saw her breathing change from carefully controlled and measured to shuddering, he silently shifted positions. Shifters were known for their ability to move soundlessly when they were in wolf form, and for most of them, it was a skill easily transferred to their human side. Watching over her felt right, and the longer he stood beside her, the harder it was to maintain the distance. The second time her shoulders shook, he heard her small hiccup as her tears continued to fall. *Fuck giving her space.*

"No, baby. Don't cry." He was on the bed beside her before she'd even known he was close. Smoothing his hand over the side of her face, Trin wanted to kick himself for the way the evening had gone down. Despite knowing she was going to run, he felt guilty about setting her up to fail. He'd scared her out of her mind when it hadn't been necessary. There wasn't a chance in hell she could have gotten her car out of the garage, and the point he'd been trying to make had been completely lost in her panic.

Pulling his shirt over his head, Trin settled on top of the bed covers with his back against the headboard. Pulling her onto his lap, he opened the robe enough they would be skin to skin. As a Dom, he understood the importance of maintaining constant physical contact with a submissive, and as Paris' mate, he wanted her as close as possible.

"I've got you, sweetness. Let it out, baby." Her deep sobs were heart-wrenching, and Trinity worried if he didn't get her calmed down, she'd make herself sick. Pressing her against his bare chest seemed to be calming the storm, but he could still sense an overwhelming sadness Paris seemed barely keeping under wraps.

"Contrary to the way it might look, I'm actually a good listener, baby." She didn't answer except to shake her head. Sighing to himself, Trinity knew he'd brought this on himself. Instead of sitting down and listening to her, the first time they were alone, he'd punished her. Fuck, she'd had the spanking coming, but the timing sucked. "Okay, let me put this another way. It makes it very difficult for me to protect you if I don't have all the information. I'm sure your brother, Israel, would tell you the same thing."

Paris slowly settled down, and Trinity breathed out a sigh of relief when he felt her relax against his chest. Within seconds, her breathing leveled out, and he knew she'd finally fallen asleep. Exhaustion had won the battle. He'd hold her all night if it meant she was well rested for their conversation tomorrow. Trinity mentally prepared for what was shaping up to be a long night. He knew he needed to check in with his office and update London's family. It was possible one of them knew more about what happened in California. Thankfully his phone was within reach, and he was able to do everything without waking Paris.

As he was setting his phone on the nightstand, he saw a message from one of his deputies. It seemed one of the men watching the clinic compound had gotten too close to the electrified portion of the fence. Trinity was barely able to contain his laughter—served the bastard right. Messaging back, Trinity asked, *Is he all right?* His deputy's response was accompanied by several laughing face emojis.

Hope he is being well paid.

ISRAEL ADLER GLARED at the string of messages on his phone. It never paid to be off the grid for any length of time because he inevitably returned to a mess. Israel needed to either cut back on the number of cases he accepted or hire help. Neither option held much appeal, but he'd seen investigators burn-out and was starting to recognize some of those same symptoms in himself. Scrolling through the messages, Israel zeroed in on one from Ian McGregor, mentioning the tracking bracelet he'd made for Paris. *What the fuck? Paris? My sister, Paris?*

Wading through the slew of messages, Israel felt his

blood pressure spike when he thought about his youngest sister dealing with a stalker. Adding insult to fucking injury, the man was her closest friend. The urge to shift and run off his anger was so overwhelming, Israel had to stand and walk it off. Shifting into his wolf on an airport concourse wasn't anything he even wanted to think about. Moving to the airline counter, Israel started the arduous task of changing his flight itinerary. Once he landed in New York, he'd head to Boston instead of flying on to Houston.

Fucking hell, my life has turned into a sappy country western song.

Chapter Eleven

PARIS SAT STRAIGHT up in bed, gasping for breath. Something was wrong. Something had changed. "Who's there?" She barely recognized her own voice it sounded shrill and panicked.

"It's just me, Sprite. Trinity. I'm the only one here. I just left the room to shower. Are you all right?" His voice came from behind her, causing Paris to turn so quickly, she nearly fell off the bed.

"Why is it so dark in here? It wasn't this dark when I went to sleep. Oh, my Goddess, I've overslept and missed my meeting with Elijah." Scrambling to untangle herself from the sheet, she tipped precariously over the edge of the bed again before she felt strong fingers grasp her upper arms.

"It's dark in here because I pulled the shades and closed the drapes so you could sleep a while longer. You needed the rest, baby. I'll take you to Eli's office after you've eaten, he's expecting you in one hour. We'll talk while we eat. Now, I'd appreciate it if you wouldn't fall out of bed. Evan and Elijah would skin me alive if I showed up with you battered and bruised."

"I think you are exaggerating the level of affection my

new brothers-in-law feel for me. We barely know each other. Almost all of our interaction has been related to either Brooklyn's hospitalization or them hooking up with London."

"Hooking up? I can promise you they would take exception to that particular phrase. It implies their relationship with their lovely mate is something tawdry."

"Oh. My. Heavenly. Goddess. And. Goat. Balls. Did you just say *tawdry*? Holy hell, I didn't know anyone used that word anymore. How old are you anyway?" Paris saw Trinity stiffen for just a moment before he grinned at her.

"Old enough to know your pretty ass is probably too sore for another paddling, so you better stop stalling. You have twenty minutes to shower, dress, and get down to the kitchen." Picking her up and setting her on her feet, he gave her bare ass—*hey, what happened to my robe*—a swat that sent her up on her toes. Paris turned once she was out of reach, looking for her phone, her gaze swept over the bedside table and dresser.

"If you are looking for your phone, I took it downstairs. The damn thing was about to vibrate itself off the table. You'll have time to return all those messages after your meeting with Eli, which you are going to miss if you don't get a move on."

A lot of messages could only mean one thing—her siblings knew about David. *Dandy.* She was tempted to start a betting pool on which one of them would be the most pissed off she hadn't told them what was happening. *The pool is out because you don't know enough people here to fleece... you'd do better to bet on how long until someone drops a net over you for talking to yourself.*

She was in and out of the shower in record time. The last thing she wanted was to be late for her meeting with Eli. Most of the graduates she knew were frantically applying for jobs all over the country, so she knew how lucky she was to have secured the plum position setting up a new school. Getting in on the ground floor, helping design the curriculum to ensure the pack's children had every possible educational advantage was going to be a dream come true.

Skidding around the corner a few minutes later, Paris skirted one wall only to run into another—the second one might be flesh and bone, but it was every bit as hard as the first.

"Damn, baby, where's the fire?"

"Sorry, I'm hungry... and I tend to be pretty focused when it comes to food." Trinity pulled her against his chest, his chuckle vibrating all the way to her empty stomach, which growled in response.

"Come on, I was just coming to get you—breakfast is ready." Sitting down at the small table in the kitchen, Paris stared at the feast Trinity had set out. "Don't look so surprised, Sprite. I've lived on my own for a long time—I had to learn to cook or starve."

"I lived in a condo during college. Thanks to Austin's negotiations and brilliant management skills, I didn't have to share the space. Of course, if I'd had a roommate, maybe she would have taught me how to cook." It was probably best to keep quiet about the visits the local fire department made to her condo.

Paris hadn't been kidding about Austin's negotiation skills... he'd gotten a phenomenal property for a reasonable price, and his regular donations to the homeowner's association kept them from kicking her to the curb. Laughing to herself, she remembered her friends teasing her that the complex's new splash park should be named after her big brother. Paris hadn't made many friends in California and looking back, she realized it was in large part because David had monopolized her time.

"Talk to me, Paris." Trinity's soft entreaty pulled her back to the present, and the man sitting close enough, their knees were touching.

"I started thinking about cooking, and that led me to... well, it eventually led me to think about why I didn't make a lot of friends in California. I met David at freshman orientation, and we became fast friends. Looking back, I can see a lot of things that should have tipped me off, but at the time, I was grateful for a friend when I felt so isolated from my family. It should have occurred to me it was too good to be true, but it didn't."

"What do you mean by too good to be true?"

"All my life, I've dealt with so-called *friends* who were more interested in gaining access to one of my brothers or sisters than they were in being pals with me. After Kenz became a household name, it was even worse." Her famous brother was one of the reasons Paris had been happy to have a male friend after discovering most of her circle in high school had only befriended her in hopes of meeting her tall, dark, and handsome brother. Kensington Adler was a global superstar—movies, television, stage— the entire world was his for the taking. Waving her hands, trying to dismiss the unpleasant memories, Paris quickly ate a couple more bites, moaning in pleasure.

"Mercy, you are going to make someone a wonderful wife someday, Trinity." The air around her seemed to crackle with electricity, making the hair on the back of her neck stand on end. Slowly raising her eyes to meet his, Paris realized the significance of her teasing words. "You know it's just an expression, right?"

"I am a top. I will not ever be anyone's *wife*. One of the hallmarks of the lifestyle is the understanding and acceptance of others' kinks. What happens between consenting adults is between them. Safe, sane, and consensual is more than a slogan, baby—it's the guiding tenet we all live by." He paused for a moment before giving her a wicked grin. "Besides, I much prefer the term gourmet chef if you don't mind." She sighed in relief when the storm brewing seemed to pass, amusement taking its place.

The next several minutes passed in comfortable silence while they enjoyed their breakfast. By the time she finally pushed her plate away and leaned back sighing in sated bliss, Paris realized Trinity was studying her.

"Help me understand your reaction last night. It was extreme by anyone's standard. Tell me what triggered it so we can avoid a repeat." Pulling in a deep breath, Paris nodded her understanding. "If it helps, think of me as an investigating officer, go that route."

"I'll try, but to be honest, I'm not sure I can…" *disassociate myself from my personal feelings for you.* Trinity's knowing smile told her he'd understood her unspoken words.

AND I'LL TRY to keep my rage concealed. Hiding his anger at what Paris had endured was harder than Trinity anticipated and knowing she'd been in the midst of this cluster the first time he'd stopped her for speeding made him wish he'd asked more questions during their encounter. He'd attributed her evasive answers to her desperation to keep him from calling her brother, but since the rental car was in Austin's name, Trinity had called him anyway. *Why didn't I ask why the vehicle was in another name—especially since Austin's address was Texas, and little Mario Adler had a California driver's license?*

"Everything started with notes and flowers. Looking back, I should have been more suspicious that the odd gifts were from someone who knew me because the flowers were always something I'd mentioned recently. It was the same with the gifts. If I admired something while strolling down the street with my friends, I'd return to my condo and find it waiting outside my door, which was pretty scary because some of the gifts were valuable."

"The gifts were left outside your door rather than inside your home?"

"Yes... well, for the first six or seven months. Then I walked in late one night to find a small basket on my dining room table."

Trinity watched her hands begin to shake but resisted the urge to wrap his long fingers around them, knowing any move on his part would break the flow of conversation, and her reaction told him this was a significant incident. Whatever she was about to share had been a big part of whatever triggered her over the top reaction last night.

"Even though I was exhausted from traveling, I was skeptical enough to shake the basket before I opened it." Her shudder seemed to start at her core before working its way to the surface. "My parents traveled a lot, but by the time I was in junior high school, they were settled in Texas. Being a Texas girl means I recognize the sound of a rattlesnake when I hear it. That was the first time I called the police. Since I had no way of knowing if there were other snakes inside, I had to vacate the condo for several days while it was checked."

"Where did you stay?" Trinity hated the growl he heard in his own voice. The crease between her brows assured him he already knew the answer.

"I called David, and *miraculously,* he was only a few blocks away."

It was easy to hear the cynicism in her voice. As the Sheriff, he'd heard the same self-censure in victims' voices before. He always tried to remind people hindsight was twenty-twenty, but it rarely made any difference. Since Trin didn't have any reason to believe Paris would be different, he kept the bit of wisdom to himself.

"I should have been suspicious when he wasn't afraid to go inside and pack a bag for me. Fuzzy bunny nuts, the cops couldn't get out of there fast enough. They said they dusted for prints, but I'm sure they didn't. Asshats."

"But David was your knight in shining armor." Trinity sucked in a calming breath and apologized. "I'm sorry, that was out of line. I'm just pissed about the fear I felt coming off you in waves last night. My bitterness is aimed at him, not you." He watched her eyes fill with tears, but she bravely blinked them away before continuing.

"David has a really nice penthouse apartment with several guest bedrooms. I chose the one farthest from the master bedroom to give him privacy. Since I'd never seen him with a woman, but he talked about *dates*, I assumed he was gay. I found out later, the *dates* he'd been talking about were the times we'd gone out for dinner or to a movie. Over the past year or so, David managed to completely isolate me from the few female friends I had by telling me things he'd overheard them saying about me, etc." Shaking her head, Paris seemed to be thinking aloud when she quietly added, "A couple of those women tried to warn me about David, but I didn't listen."

Trinity hoped his sweet mate would get a chance to talk with her friends again, it would go a long way to ease the regret he could see in her eyes. He admired the way she shook off her melancholy with remarkable determination—Paris was so much stronger than she knew. He looked forward to helping her realize her full potential.

During the next several minutes, Paris described several more incidents, each one with a common thread—David Lamb was conveniently nearby and happy to come to her rescue. Trinity knew she'd been distracted with finals and wrapping up the paperwork for graduation, but it was a surprise she hadn't started to suspect the one person who was always close when things went down.

"I know what you're thinking, and you're right... I should have figured it out. Maybe somewhere in the back of my mind I did because when my car suddenly wouldn't start after I returned from a visit here, I called Kensington since I knew he was in town, and he sent a driver to take me home. Before I could call the auto club, Kenz had already taken care of it, and let me tell you, big brother was not happy someone had sabotaged my car."

Trinity felt his blood pressure start to spike and wondered if he should have broken this conversation up into more manageable segments. Hell, at this rate, he was going to have a fucking stroke. Before she could continue, his phone chimed with an incoming message.

"That was Eli. He's available earlier than he expected." Holding out his hand, he purposely relaxed his stance and smoothed out his expression. "Come." She put her small hand in his, letting him pull her to her feet. "Let's go get you officially hired, then we'll come back to celebrate. You can tell me the rest of the story in the cart." Hopefully, he wouldn't drive the damned supped-up golf cart into the tunnel wall.

By the time Paris touched up her make-up, brushed her teeth—again, and grabbed her purse, Trinity was standing by the elevator, rolling his eyes. She'd left him cooling his heels for ten minutes, then laughed when she saw him.

"You look like one of those cartoon characters with steam coming out their ears."

"There's no steam coming from my ears, but it's not out of the realm of possibility." Laughing at his own impatience, Trin realized how long it had been since he'd been forced to wait for a woman. *Isn't there a country song about waiting for a woman?* "I will say, the past few minutes gives me a new appreciation for my dad's frustration waiting for my mom—who always seemed to keep us waiting before leaving the house." He chuckled as they exited the elevator into the tunnel. He hadn't thought about his dad's exasperation about his mom's lack of respect for time in a long time.

Before starting the cart, Trinity turned to Paris and

shook his head. "Don't fidget, Sprite. You look amazing, and you've already got the job, this is just details." He saw her take a deep breath and nod.

"Thanks. It's nice knowing I have someone in my corner. As much as I hate everything David did and the horrible way things ended..." Paris stared straight ahead for several seconds before meeting his gaze. "This will sound ridiculous, but I miss his friendship. Even though I know nothing about it was what it seemed, it's still hard to lose my best friend."

"Baby, it makes perfect sense. You miss the person you *thought* you knew. It's Lamb's fault that man didn't really exist." Thankfully, the tears he'd seen shining in her eyes disappeared, and Paris gave him a small smile. She might not understand her feelings about David Lamb, but Trinity understood how difficult it could be to move on from a betrayal. Starting the cart and moving down the tunnel, he wondered if perhaps it would be better to let her tell him the rest of the story in her own time rather than forcing the issue. As if she'd read his mind, Paris turned to him and smiled.

"I don't want this hanging over my head during my meeting with Elijah, so I'm just going to blurt it out." Trinity admired her grit; the woman didn't back away from a challenge. "David knew I was leaving to come here before flying to the Caribbean. He tried to finagle an invitation to London's wedding, but something kept holding me back." *Baby, that's called going with your gut, I'm glad you heeded the warning.* Waving her small hand as if clearing away another obstacle, Paris continued, "Anyway, he was clearly annoyed when he left my condo. The whole thing was sort of baffling. Even though we had attended family events together, we'd always gone as friends, never as a couple. While I finished packing and loading everything in my car, I kept replaying the evening in my head. I remembered something he'd said about you and chills went up my spine."

"Me? How did he... oh, you'd talked about me with your best friend. Gotcha. Was he pissed about the speeding tickets?"

"No." Her blunt answer confused him. "He'd figured out I was... well, I am attracted to you. He called our bickering foreplay and accused me of coming here before the wedding so I could... and I quote, *fuck the hick sheriff.*"

Trinity worked to keep his anger in check. While he was thrilled to know she'd been attracted to him, it pissed him off to know Lamb had berated her for admitting as much to someone she considered a friend. It was probably going to be a long time before she was able to trust enough to form a similar bond.

"I locked up the condo, took a shower, and fell into bed. I was so exhausted, I didn't even bother with a nightgown. The whole evening had been such a nightmare, I could feel a headache building, so I'd taken a couple aspirin. I'm particularly sensitive to pain medications—heck, I usually sleep for hours after taking one low-dose aspirin—but I knew I had to head off the migraine if I was going to be able to drive into the rising sun the next morning."

They'd reached their destination, but Trin didn't want to interrupt her story, so he parked off to the side and sent a telepathic message to Elijah letting him know what was happening. The meeting was important, but finding out what they were dealing with was crucial. Protecting Paris from a man with the financial and political resources David Lamb had at his fingertips wasn't something any of them were taking lightly.

"I don't know what woke me up, maybe some inner sense of self-preservation. By the time the fog from the aspirin cleared enough for me to assess the situation, David was already on top of the bed covers, straddling me. I swear it was like he'd turned into someone else entirely. It was terrifying. He'd tried to trap my arms against my sides, but I managed to wiggle free while he was screaming about how ungrateful I was and how he was willing to give me everything my heart desired. He yelled about all the gifts he'd sent and how I knew it was him all along—he said we'd been doing a mating dance, and he had too much invested in me to let me go."

Trinity was impressed by her composure and guessed she was using detachment to her advantage. He wouldn't object to Paris shutting down her emotions to get through the next couple of hours, but long-term emotional distance would be devastating to someone with a sensitive soul. Allowing her to exist in an emotional vacuum wouldn't just shield her from the fear, it would also rob her of life's joys.

"It seems weird now, but at the time, all I could think of was how strange it was he thought I'd even consider being with him after everything he'd done. Thankfully, I knew he spent a lot of time in the gym but has never trained in any of the martial arts." Trinity felt himself smile for the first time since this damned story started.

Chapter Twelve

"That wasn't the longest meeting I've ever attended, but it felt like it," Paris sighed, leaning back against the cart's seat. "Holy crap on a crown, Elijah Monroe is a force to be reckoned with. It's a good thing London is brilliant." She knew the smile spreading over her face was part relief and part amusement. "I wonder if Elijah and Evan know what they've gotten themselves in to. They bravely marry and mate with one of the best researchers in the country, then hire her crazy sister."

Trinity turned the cart so quickly, she nearly slid off the seat. Parking in a small alcove, Trinity pulled her close, crashing his mouth down on hers. Growling deep in his chest, he ravaged her mouth in a kiss that screamed possession and unrelenting need. She felt his hand snake under her shirt to cup her breast. Groaning, Paris arched into his touch. *I wonder if he could make me come just by playing with my breasts?*

"I can smell your need, baby, and I plan on giving you exactly what you want, but first we need to talk."

Talk? He wants to talk? Now? I thought it was supposed to be women who wanted to talk all the time.

"We can talk later. After..." Paris couldn't believe he'd

pulled back. What the hell had he been thinking when he'd started something he didn't plan to finish? *Can you say irony? The man I wanted as a friend wants more, and the one I crave seems to be happy keeping me at arm's length.*

"After?" Paris could have sworn she heard laughter in his voice despite his stoic expression.

"Are you laughing at me? Because if you're laughing, that's going to rain on my parade, and I'd have to go into the city and indulge in a bit of retail therapy."

"You're not going anywhere except upstairs to the playroom. Now, about that chat. You will not refer to yourself as crazy. You're smart, witty, gorgeous, and *mine!*"

Paris felt the telltale burning at the back of her eyes and tried unsuccessfully to blink back the tears. Trinity pressed a kiss to her forehead and gave her nipple a sharp pinch before withdrawing his hand.

"Don't speak about yourself disparagingly, or there will be consequences next time. Now, let's go. We need to celebrate, and I've got a plan."

PARIS STARED AT him from the St. Andrew's Cross where he'd bound her, confusion rather than desire glittering in her blue eyes. Trinity knew he'd thrown her for a loop when he'd pulled back, down in the tunnel, but he also knew every inch of the underground passageway was monitored. He would enjoy showing Paris off at the club or a private party, but he didn't want her pleasure displayed for the security team. Despite being shifters, who are by nature very sexual creatures, they were still a part of a tightly knit community where gossip could spread at the speed of sound—literally.

"You are beautiful, Sprite. Seeing you displayed for my enjoyment fills me with anticipation. I know you've been on edge since our encounter in the tunnel, and I want you to know how pleased I am by your patience." Hell, he was damned impressed she hadn't clawed his eyes out. It wasn't her reputation as impulsive he'd thought might send her over the edge in the tunnel, it was the tidal wave of need he'd felt rolling off her. They were becoming more connected, making him wonder how much stronger their link would be after he claimed her.

"Your compliance pleases me more than you know, baby." Damn, he was proud of her. He'd outlined his expectations before they entered the playroom and so far, she'd done beautifully. "I know your experience in the lifestyle is limited, which makes the way you handled your frustration in the tunnel even more impressive." He knew Paris wasn't convinced she could be what he wanted, but she couldn't be more off the mark.

Walking around her with slow purpose, Trinity made certain he maintained some level of physical contact when he was out of her sight. Whether he was trailing the soft deer-skin leather strips of his favorite flogger over her drool-inducing curves or stroking the pads of his calloused fingers up and down her spine, he relished the way goose flesh followed his touch.

"You are so responsive, baby. Before I spin you up, I want to ask you a question." She needed to make this decision with as clear a mind as possible. *I've already pushed this seduction farther than I should have—but I didn't want there to be any chance she'd say no.* Trinity wouldn't use sexual seduction to persuade her to submit to the mating bite, but he wasn't above using sensual luring. *Go ahead and keep telling yourself those aren't two sides of the same coin, asshole.*

"Tell me what you know about mating in shifters, Paris." She looked surprised by the question but covered quickly. It was fascinating to see her refocus her attention on the question he'd asked, despite being bound naked in front of a man she wanted as much as he wanted her. The question was—would she be brave enough to admit it?

"I don't know much aside from shifters are fiercely loyal and mate for life. They are also not averse to polyamorous marriages." She stopped suddenly, seeming to consider the implications of what she'd said. "Okay, so that's marriage, and I don't know if that's synonymous with mating or not."

"It is. But what I was asking was, what do you know about the *process*?" The light in her eyes brightened as his meaning registered.

"Oh, I don't know much, but I could make an educated guess since I noticed two small scars on the upper slope of both London's shoulders. They are round, like puncture wounds. They're flat, so they must have healed quickly... probably bite marks. So, it seems reasonable to assume that's at least a part of the mating process." He smiled to himself. Damn, it appeared Paris was as astute as he'd have expected.

Standing in front of her so he could meet her gaze, Trinity tucked the handle of the flogger under one arm, using his fingers to roll her pale pink nipples between his fingers until they peaked, turning a lovely shade of rose.

Giving the nubs a sharp pinch, he smiled when her back bowed. He hadn't left her much room for movement, the bindings were fairly snug, but she'd still managed to push her breasts closer in offering.

"Biting where the shoulder and neck join is a centuries-old tradition. The marks heal completely in a matter of seconds but remain visible as a sign to other shifters the female is mated—although it's purely symbolic since your body chemistry will change, and every shifter will know you are my mate."

Trinity knew he'd changed from speaking, in general, to specifically about the two of them. His wickedly smart mate hadn't missed the subtle switch. Watching her eyes dilate until only a thin ring of blue remained, along with the rapid rise and fall of her chest as her respiration kicked into high gear was the most enchanting thing he'd ever seen.

"You are mine, Paris. I knew you were my mate the first time I stopped you for speeding." Knowing his mate had put herself in such danger had scared the hell out of him, and he'd lashed out at her in the process.

"You want to bite me?" Trinity looked on as a shudder skittered up her spine, a reaction he knew was equal parts apprehension and anticipation. "I don't know... that sounds painful, and I'm not really into pain." Trinity had to fight back his smile—this was the woman whose body was arching into his stinging touch, the one whose scent filled the room. He planned to show her just how much she enjoyed pain.

"Pleasure and pain are two sides of the same coin, and I'm looking forward to showing you how much you enjoy the edge of pain—how much it can ramp up your enjoyment if you put yourself in my hands, Sprite. Watching you arch closer when I pinch your swollen nipples, the way your pussy floods with cream—oh yeah, baby, your body responds perfectly to a bit of pain." Trinity paused long enough for Paris to absorb the words. Her eyes were starting to get the soft, glazed look he loved seeing in a sub's expression.

"Tell me you want to belong to me, Paris. We are meant to be." He knew he was rushing her, but the truth was, he was worried about her running or worse, being taken out from under his nose. After they were mated, he'd be able to find her easily. Mating would likely enhance her ability to defend herself as well, and if she gained the ability to shift—all the better.

"I don't think you know what you're getting in to... and I'm pretty sure my brothers and sisters would tell you the same thing." Trinity didn't respond, simply waited while she mulled over what else to say. Watching her bite her lip, Trinity could almost hear the rush of thoughts streaming through her mind.

"I don't think I'll be a good mate, and I'm sure you have plenty of women who would love to be your submissive... women who really are submissive." It amused him she didn't consider herself submissive when it was blatantly obvious to him. "I don't understand why you want me, Trinity... Sir. I'm just starting my career; my brother controls my money until I'm thirty or I marry."

"My interest in you has nothing to do with your career—although I am looking forward to watching you grow in your chosen field. Nor am I interested in your money. We haven't discussed it, but I work because I want to, not because it's necessary. I founded Deep Frost, a cybersecurity company when I was in college, I retained ownership, but no longer manage the day to day operations. I used my mother's family name for years to avoid being linked to the fashion label my parents own."

It had taken several years for the paperwork to be completed for his team to manage Deep Frost, but once everything was in place, he'd finally returned to his father's name. Using the name long associated with magical families had settled something inside Trinity, and he'd finally felt he was ready for a new stage in his life. Shrugging, he gave her a quick grin before continuing.

"The bottom line is… I don't need your money, Sprite. I'd prefer you left the investments with your brother after we're married. You'll feel better knowing it's there, and I'll feel better knowing you'd have instant access to cash if anything happened to me." She'd be a very wealthy woman, but it would take time to sell his interests in both companies. *Substantial assets are rarely liquid.*

"Holy haggard handmaids, that was the worst proposal in history."

Of all the things Trinity had expected Paris to say, that wasn't even on the list. Trin burst out laughing, then shook his head. Damn if she wasn't right. *When is the last time a sub made you laugh during a scene? Never. Fucking hell, she's perfect.* For the first time in years, Trinity realized he'd become far too serious. When had he forgotten how to have fun? To laugh at the little things in life? When he hadn't been raising hell in high school, he'd been busy writing code. After starting his business, he'd hired the best people to run it and devoted himself to raising hell—until a pack elder assigned him to shadow the local Sheriff.

"You're right, baby. I promise to up my game, and we'll have a redo on the proposal." He'd make it a proposal she'd never forget. He had a secret weapon—her sister was less than a mile away and still floating in honeymoon bliss. Trinity knew London would be happy to provide guidance.

"You haven't answered my question, Sprite. I want to claim you, but I won't until you agree. You are my mate, and I am convinced you can feel the electricity arcing between us."

"I can feel it. It's a bit overwhelming at times. You are so much more experienced, I worry it'll be impossible to learn enough... fast enough, to keep your interest. And even though I want to belong to you, I need to know you won't go bananas the first time I sass back or drive."

"Drive too fast, my sweet mate, and I can promise there will be consequences." Trinity didn't hesitate to interrupt. Paris' safety was the one area where he would never compromise. She was already being threatened, and he was struggling to cope with the elements of danger he couldn't control. Leaving her to waltz knowingly into a potential threat wasn't happening.

"Maybe I'll ask Bronx to get me a granny car." Her overly dramatic sigh of resignation was amusing.

"That's cheating, Sprite," he teased. Wrapping his hand around the back of her neck, cupping the base of her skull, Trinity massaged the tight muscles, pleased when she moaned softly. "I'll help you learn control, baby."

We'll have many, many years together to work through the challenges.

Chapter Thirteen

Two Days Later

ISRAEL ADLER STARED at the screen watching for any indication Ian McGregor and Luke Grayson were wrong. The chances two of the smartest men he knew had made the same mistake were somewhere between slim and non-existent. Unfortunately, it was the only hope he had.

"Pull her in? What the fuck?" He couldn't believe Senator Lamb wanted the FBI to bring Paris in for questioning. "What's the basis? Questioning about what for Goddess' sake?" Hell, his blood pressure was going to give him a stroke if he didn't get some damned help hired.

"It's a power play because Paris filed a complaint against David Lamb for breaking and entering an occupied residence, sexual assault, and battery." Luke chuckled and shook his head. "Although they might have a hard time making the last one stick since she beat the shit out of the little fucker. Damn, I'm proud of her, and B is practically beaming."

"This happened before the wedding, and she didn't say a damned word to anybody? I hope to hell Trinity has shown her the error of her ways." The smiles on Ian's and

Luke's faces assured Israel his sister probably wasn't sitting comfortably. Shaking his head, Israel realized for the first time he was thinking of Paris as an adult—*Damn, she grew up while I wasn't paying attention.*

"It seems the good Senator wants to chat with Paris. And since the team she sent to pull your sister in hasn't been able to get through Evan's security—she's playing the power card." Luke was talking but never stopped typing on the keyboard in front of him—*amazing.* "We were watching the son, not the mother, so the old bat got ahead of us, but she's suddenly having trouble getting her paperwork to go through.

"Challenging Nancy Lamb doesn't come without potential problems." Ian leaned forward for emphasis, and Israel knew where the conversation was headed. Anyone holding the Senate seat Nancy Lamb had called her own for two decades, was well accustomed to getting their way. When denied, they tended to dig their heels in and go down with the ship.

"You and Ian are on the same page. He thinks the old bitty will go to war before she backs off, so we're going to distract her, then re-route this fucking train wreck to the FBI Headquarters in D.C." Israel gave his friends a broad smile, he knew several ranking members of the FBI were long-standing members of Club Isola, they could interview Paris under Ian's watchful eye.

"You're consulting with the local Sheriff?" Israel knew it was a given but felt obligated to ask, anyway.

"He got the long version this morning, you're getting the abbreviated update because we both have sweet submissives we're anxious to get back to. All work and no play makes me cranky." Israel laughed at Ian's confession because he could remember when his friend was so obsessed with work no one who knew him thought he'd ever find a submissive of his own.

A flash of emptiness hit Israel fast and hard, but it was gone just as quickly. Sucking in a startled breath when he felt the warm brush of fingers over his cheek, Israel knew he would recognize the caress anywhere. His mother always stroked his cheek with the backs of her fingers when she knew he was worried or stressed. Taking another deep breath, Israel refocused on the present.

"I'm in New York, I'm taking Catalina to dinner tonight and will catch an early flight tomorrow. Do you have a room available, or do I need to stay in the city." He hoped like hell one of the small apartments in the club would be open—and one close to where Ian was planning to stash Paris would be even better.

"Already taken care of. You'll have the suite next to Paris and Trinity. Don't be surprised if you see the Wests wandering the halls." Ian grinned before adding, "Lilly and Tobi planned a shopping trip in D.C. and New York." Israel knew his surprise must have shown in his expression because Ian laughed out loud. "Not to worry, their men are not unleashing them on the east coast unattended. I'm pleased Del and Dean will be here to act as advisors. They'll provide a much-needed buffer. You can't replace experience when assessing situations the rest of us refer to as FUBAR, these men are particularly skilled when it comes to finding solutions we might have missed."

"I agree. There's no substitute for experience, I've heard they are both remarkable strategists." Israel had heard his military friends use the term FUBAR and knew it meant fucked up beyond all recognition, but it was the first time he'd heard Ian admit there were times he sought guidance from anyone other than Daniel Lamont. Daniel and Catherine Lamont's sons, Alex and Zach owned The ShadowDance Club in Colorado. ShadowDance was similar to Prairie Winds, Club Isola, and Mountain Masters because all the owners were friends before starting their individual kink clubs. People often joked about Club Isola catering to a kinkier crowd because of its proximity to the nation's capital. As far as Israel was concerned, it wasn't a joke—it was the fucking gospel. The ultra-exclusive club was the only safe place for the rich and powerful to enjoy their kink without worrying the prying eyes of the press or their political enemies were lurking around the corner, ready to use the information against them.

"The Wests are due to arrive later today. Callie has planned a dinner party, and I want to spin her up a bit before we sit down for what I hope will be a very enjoyable meal. Luke will email you a run-down. Will Cooper be joining you for dinner?" Israel hadn't considered the possibility, but now it seemed likely. He'd learned a long time ago, Ian McGregor didn't ask random questions. When he simply raised a brow in question, Ian shrugged.

"Just in case, please update him as well. I'll have a suite ready for them." Damn, McGregor was assembling a hell of a group of operatives and strategists. He was front-loading in a big way, making Israel anxious to read the documentation he knew Luke had already sent.

Israel watched Ian's attention shifted to something or someone out of camera range—when the club owner's eyes dilated, it didn't take a genius to know Callie had entered her husband's office. Watching the change in the owner of Club Isola was fascinating—his expression went from happy greeting to blazing desire between one heartbeat and the next. Ian pulled his naked wife onto his lap, smiling at her indulgently. Israel noted Luke had stopped typing, the silence falling eerily around them. There was something so captivating about Callie McGregor everything seemed to go into slow motion for a few seconds whenever she entered the room.

One night, well, actually the final hour before dawn, after a particularly wild night at the club, Israel had joined a small group of Doms decompressing in the bar area. The conversation turned to contracts between Dominants and Submissives—how valuable are they in the long run? What's the ideal length of time? The conversation had been lively, considering they were all beat, but Ian had noticeably stayed out of the discussion. When one of the Dungeon Monitors asked him to weigh in, the boss had shaken his head and smiled.

"If Callie had shown up on the dock and you'd been the first one on the scene, would you have taken a chance with a contract, or would you have simply collared her?" The other man nodded his head once in acknowledgment. The boss was right. "Have you ever noticed that time stops—just for a second when she walks into the room. It's fucking remarkable. I've watched it time and again—it doesn't matter if it's the club, a restaurant, or group of moms from Carly's playgroup—everything stops. Would any of you risk losing her? I didn't build my business by making foolish choices, gentlemen."

Israel would never forget the look on the men's faces and often wondered if he'd ever find a woman he recognized as his, the moment they met. He'd played with subs he considered collaring, but he'd never experienced that moment of instant recognition he knew Ian was talking about. The same warm brush of fingers caressed his cheek again, his mother's soft voice moving through his mind. *Soon, sweetheart. Very soon.*

PARIS COULDN'T BELIEVE she and Trinity were on their way to Club Isola. When she'd first started researching the lifestyle, it was the club all others seemed to aspire to emulate. Callie McGregor had invited her to visit; unfortunately, this wasn't the social call Paris had envisioned. While she was grateful for Ian McGregor's help, knowing she'd landed on Senator Lamb's bad side didn't bode well for her future.

The small ferry they'd boarded bumped gently against the dock and Paris smiled when she saw Callie and Abby waving from the edge of the wooden structure. Their men were standing behind them, legs spread, arms crossed over their impressive chests, looking like indulgent sentinels. Oh, make no mistake Ian McGregor, Logan Douglas, and Kalen Black were all three Doms from the tops of their heads to the tips of their booted feet. Paris wrapped her hand around the top rail, ready to hop over onto the dark decking of the dock when Trinity grasped the back of her shirt, stopping her.

"Where do you think you're going, Beautiful?" Trinity

leaned down, licking the two small scars at the top of her left shoulder. The touch was so blatantly sexual, Paris felt her body respond with the familiar fire starting in her core before igniting every cell it touched as the heat moved at the speed of light through her. Damn it, her knees were threatening to fold out from under her... *again.*

How long is this going to last? Goddess above, when am I going to regain control of my own body? Since he'd claimed her two nights ago, Paris hadn't been able to control her response to Trinity. Hell, all she had to do was catch a whiff of his scent, and her sex flooded with cream. She'd changed panties so many times, Paris felt like she'd spent more time doing laundry than working on plans for the new school.

"The intensity of our mutual attraction will remain at this level until the next full moon. It'll slowly fade to a more manageable level in the coming months, but we'll always experience a magnetic draw stronger than what you'd expect to find in non-shifter relationships. Your scent is imprinted on the most primal part of my being. I could track you anywhere in the world, mate." His fingers traced the tracking bracelet, licking the shell of her ear then caught her when her knees folded. Trinity had effectively distracted her long enough for the crew to set up a safe exit a few feet from where she'd been ready to climb the rail.

"You did that on purpose, didn't you? Don't forget I spent the last five years in California, I know how to hop a rail and secure a line." She'd spent so much time at the marina when she'd first moved to the west coast, the locals adopted her as they would a stray pet. The entire area had a laid-back vibe she'd found soothing, and since it was just down the block from her condo, Paris loved studying at one of the many outdoor cafes and picnic areas.

"Yes, I did it on purpose. Seducing you is so much more fun than commanding you to wait. Your safety is my top priority, sweet mate. You belong to me, and I take care of what's mine." He straightened, giving her a chance to push back some of the need barreling through her system.

"Come on, come on. Damn, I thought you two were going to spontaneously combust. You're going to give Ian and Callie a run for their money when it comes to public porno." Abby's excited voice carried easily on the breeze, making Paris giggle.

"Baby, you'd better rein it in a bit before your other Master has a stroke." Logan's tone might have sounded teasing, but one look at Kalen told Paris the warning had been real. The man with the angelic voice looked even more formidable in person. Neither Logan's warning nor Kalen's appeared to have any effect on Abby as she rushed forward to give Paris a rib-crushing hug.

"Love, you're hurting her. Not everyone is a Tinkerbell Ninja warrior. Let Paris take a breath before her knees fold out from under her—*again*." Kalen winked at Paris, and for the first time, she understood what nineteenth-century authors meant when they talked about a woman swooning. A heated flush blazed over her cheeks, and she could have sworn she heard Trinity growl.

"Oh, pickle fudge. Sorry, I get excited and forget not everybody grew up surrounded by Special Forces operators who took great delight in teaching me how to snap people like twigs."

"Something we've come to regret, I assure you." Logan grinned at his wife while extending his hand to Paris. "It's nice to meet you in person, Paris. We've heard a lot of wonderful things about you and look forward to helping you get through this mess so you can focus on your new life." While she appreciated the sentiment, Paris wasn't convinced it was going to be easy. From what she knew about Senator Lamb, the woman was relentless when it came to getting what she felt she was entitled to. And, for some reason, the barracuda seemed intent on having Paris' head on a platter.

Ian stepped forward to greet her with a quick hug before setting her back, studying her carefully. His eyes never left hers, but she knew he'd cataloged even the smallest details. "Welcome to Club Isola, Paris. Callie and I are pleased you're here, even though I wish it were under different circumstances." She nodded despite feeling like she was being steamrolled by the dichotomy of Ian McGregor. Everything about him screamed wealth and class, his eyes sparkled with the intelligence of the entrepreneur she knew him to be. There was no question the man was a Dominant to the depths of his soul, and she sensed instinctively he'd been much harsher before Callie entered his life.

Stepping back, Ian motioned Callie forward. Paris was caught off guard by the petite blonde... Callie McGregor was stunning. It took Paris a few seconds to realize the other woman had apparently asked her a question. Paris heard Ian chuckle softly before leaning forward in a conspiratorial whisper, "It happens all the time, Little Light. Callie renders people speechless by simply walking into a room, it's remarkable to watch." Paris couldn't hold back her laughter, grateful Ian had rescued her. She'd even caught the reference to her being named after the City of Lights.

Callie's warm embrace settled her nerves, and before Paris realized what was happening, she found herself sandwiched between the two women as they made their way up the winding path to the club's massive stone entrance. It was easy to see why journalists were frustrated in their attempts to photograph members entering the club.

The massive door was recessed inside what appeared to be a cave opening sheltered by massive trees. The entrance would be virtually impossible to see if you weren't standing directly in front of it and any effort to use a drone would be negated by the island's security. Club Isola's proximity to the nation's capital and Ian's connections, had made it easy for him to secure a no-fly zone over the small isle. Trinity had laughed when he'd given her an overview of Jace Garrett's well-trained staff and Ian's computer wizardry.

Walking through the enormous wooden doors, Paris stopped so suddenly Trinity had to wrap his hands around her shoulders and lift her off her feet to keep from running over her. "Sorry, Sprite, I should have anticipated this reaction. It always happens with newbies." He set her gently on her feet, allowing her to step forward, exploring the vast reception area. The club wouldn't officially open for several hours, but Paris was grateful they'd arrived early. Experiencing it in stages would make it easier to take in. Knowing her brothers were members was a bit weird, but she pushed that aside and focused on the bigger issue… her new mate was also a member… of one of the most exclusive kink clubs in the country. *Holy hollyhocks!*

Chapter Fourteen

T RINITY COULD FEEL the mix of emotions coursing through his newly claimed mate and was relieved to know not one of them was related to fear. It didn't take long to complete her security pass and input her finger-prints into the system, Ian assured them Jace set it up two days earlier before returning to New York for the opening of his wife's latest screenplay. Holly, Jace, and Gage were currently on their way back to the club, and Trinity was anxious for Paris to meet her.

Holly Mills-Garrett was so multi-talented, it was hard to keep up with her newest and latest accomplishment. Trinity admired the way Jace supported his wife's goals while diplomatically trying to keep her from becoming over-extended. The two had met when she'd succumbed to the pressure and come to visit her aunt—Ian's Administra-tive Assistant Extraordinaire, Daphne Craig. With Daphne out of the office, Holly was mistaken for her temporary replacement and put to work before anyone was the wiser. By the time the mistake was discovered, Jace and Gage had already fallen for the green-eyed beauty.

Standing back, watching Paris take in everything around her, Trinity was surprised at how much her wide-eyed wonder reminded him of Holly. Desire and need clouding her bright blue eyes. Her thoughts streamed through his mind, but they were so fast and scattered he didn't have a prayer keeping up. Smiling to himself, he zeroed his focus in on the two small scars marking her as his. The wonder of their mating was quickly becoming one of his most treasured memories. Feeling the exchange of their DNA, hers racing through his veins as she'd shattered around him was beyond anything he'd ever imagined.

Callie and Abby flanked Paris, the three of them whispering, pointing, and giggling like old friends. The easy camaraderie between the trio made him chuckle. Shaking his head, Trin turned to Ian and asked, "Do you ever get used to it?" At the club owners confused look, he elaborated, "Does the new wear off? The joy of seeing the wonder in your sub's expressions—or does it always feel like a punch to the gut?" Ian's knowing smile told Trinity the man understood exactly what he was trying to say.

"You learn to manage it, but I'm happy to tell you it never fades—if it's the right woman." Ian paused for several seconds before continuing, "I know shifters have unique abilities to recognize their mates, but I think it holds true for all true soul mates. Your remarkable lifespans make it easier for you because you are up to your ass in experience." Trinity leaned his head back and laughed. Leave it to Ian to top off the Zen with a zinger of street-smart.

Trinity finally managed to get Paris into their suite—no easy task considering Callie and Abby had planned to host a little margarita party by the pool. The last thing Paris needed was to be distracted by alcohol before her first club visit. Her siblings already warned him about her low tolerance to anything with liquor. When Ian announced he was postponing their little soiree, Abby rehashed a few colorful expressions referencing his mother's marital status. Her muttering earned her several swats, which only made her more vocal.

Leaning back against the door, Trinity watched Paris bounce around the room, her excitement and exuberance reminded him how inexperienced his new mate was and how important it was going to be to hold himself back. Teaching and guidance had to take precedence.

"Sprite. Come to me." He'd already noticed how much more acute her hearing had become since their mating. She'd commented her eyesight had improved so much she'd happily flushed her contacts down the toilet. Trin watched Paris turn on the balls of her feet to return to him. The woman was grace personified, a trait that would serve her well once she learned to shift. Standing in front of him, her eyes dancing with anticipation, he watched as her pupils dilated, dominating the blue iris until only a thin halo of sapphire remained.

"Perfect. I love the way your body responds before your mind has a chance to get in the way. It pleases me more than I can say to know you're working so hard to learn and adapt to the lifestyle." And it was true—he'd been damned impressed with her efforts, but he was going to start pushing her boundaries—so the jury was still out. "Strip." The scent of her arousal instantly surrounded him, making his cock pulse against the metal teeth lining the front of his jeans. Damn, he needed to get out of his jeans before his cock was permanently marked by the fucking zipper.

Paris leaned down, slipping out of her shoes, and setting them to the side. The cornflower blue sundress he'd picked out for her matched her eyes—until they darkened with desire. The sky-blue orbs turned a deep, crystal clear sapphire as she became aroused. With a flash of insight, Trinity saw her naked, on her knees in front of him as he held a sparkling diamond and sapphire collar in his hand. The picture in his mind was so clear it was as if he was watching the scene in the woods behind the clinic compound.

Shaking off the vision, Trinity refocused his attention on the petite ball of fire currently hanging her dress over the back of a nearby chair. The white lace thong she wore framed her bare pussy perfectly, showcasing it as the work of art it was.

Using his fingers, he signaled for her to turn around slowly, whistling at the sight of her bare ass bisected by a scrap of lace. "You are so fucking beautiful, swear to Goddess you outshine every other woman in the world. You glow from the inside out, it's the damnedest thing I've ever seen."

Paris had no idea how stunning she was. She'd admitted always feeling like the ugly duckling sister, making Trinity shake his head in wonder. After claiming her, he'd made her stand in front of the large oval mirror in her bedroom, while he stood behind her, recounting in intimate detail what he saw.

"Your ass would make a Renaissance Master weep for joy, baby. Your breasts bounce perfectly when I'm fucking you, the sight of them moving in time with my thrusts is hot as hell. But it's the glow from the deepest part of your soul that will always make you beautiful. The Great Goddess's gift to you was a beauty that will never fade." He wanted her to know she would always outshine every other woman in the world in his eyes. It wasn't that he wouldn't appreciate the beautiful women who would surround them later in the club. Trinity would always appreciate beauty, whether it was the toothless smile of a six-year-old, a sunset on the beach or a dew-kissed rose in the early morning light. But no one would ever be more beautiful than the woman standing in front of him.

"Thank you, Sir." Gratitude shone in her eyes, and Trin found himself looking forward to the day when she'd be confident enough in his love, she'd accept the depth of his feelings. *How the hell do you expect her to know when you haven't told her?* The sudden realization was like being doused with ice water.

Fucking hell, he'd never told her he loved her. He'd told her in great detail what he loved about her body and how much admired her strength, but he'd never said the three little words every soul on the planet longs to hear. Closing the gap between them, Trinity framed her face with his hands, tilting her face up until he was all she could see. Her eyes fluttered shut as she anticipated his kiss, but he simply waited. When she finally opened her eyes, confusion clouding their previously bright blue depths, he shook his head.

"I love you, Paris." He wanted to kick himself at the surprise he saw flash over her heart-shaped face. "Don't ever doubt how much I love you, baby. I'll try to remember how important it is to put into words, but I want you to promise to remind me if you need to hear it." He knew she'd been holding back telling him the same, but it hadn't occurred to him why. She started to tell him several times, stopping herself each time, but her whispers while dreaming gave her away. How the hell could they be so connected, yet he'd missed such a critical piece of the puzzle?

"I love you too, Master." Trinity knew his heart skipped several beats at the honorific. Without hesitation, he pulled her against his chest, hugging her so tight he heard her squeak. Backing off enough to let her take a deep breath, Trinity felt a wave of pure joy unlike any other wash over him.

"Hearing you say the words I know you've been afraid to speak out loud was a moment I will remember for the rest of my life, baby. And, to hear you refer to me as Master was a bonus, I assure you I've dreamed of hearing. I'm going to make certain you never regret belonging to me."

"Enough to make my last speeding ticket disappear?"

"Not a chance, Sprite. Not a chance."

FUCK-A-DILLY CIRCUS. SHE should have waited until right before he was ready to come to ask. She hadn't called him Master to get out of the ticket, but Paris wasn't one to let a potential opportunity slip by either.

Damn, she could still hear Austin ripping her up one side and down the other about her latest run-in with the speed-obsessed man she was now mated to. Well, maybe she'd at least get a nice meal in jail. A sharp slap to her backside rocked Paris up onto her toes, making her yelp.

"Hey, what the holy Hannah was that for?" When she tried to reach back to sooth the burn searing her abused cheek, she was surprised to find her hands already bound in front of her. *When did he do that? Damn, I didn't go that far on my mental road trip.*

"Oh, baby, you'll find it will never take me long to secure you with some sort of bondage. I'll always have something close at hand—*always*." What on Earth had she been thinking, becoming the mate of a cop with a bondage kink? "Probably that I'm going to spend the rest of my life making certain your every licentious need is met. I'll devote myself to your pleasure, Paris." Oh, she didn't doubt that a bit... Nope, not one bit at all.

She only hoped she didn't let him down in the end. He was so much more experienced... sexually and otherwise, she worried her youthful exuberance and learn on-the-fly spirit would eventually push him away. Despite her concern, Paris wasn't willing to change who she was... not even for her hot mate. Having nine older siblings tended to make your self-esteem a sink or swim trait. She'd always credited her siblings' strong personalities with the development of her own... and there had been a lot of times it was damned hard to stand out in the crowd.

"Oh, but my sweet Paris—stand out you did. I'm going to spend the rest of my life, proving to you how truly remarkable you are." Damn it, she was going to have to get used to this telepathy thing. *Maybe London could help me learn how to shield at least some of my thoughts. Fucking hell, aren't there some kind of rules about privacy? Probably won't do me any good to Google it...and they'd just send someone to drop a net over me, anyway.* Before she had a chance to register the fact he'd moved, Trinity had her over his shoulder and was stalking down the short hall.

"I can walk, you know." *I'm noticing a pattern here.*

"I'm sure you can, but with all the nonsense racing through that beautiful head of yours, I have no damned idea how long it would take you to get there." They were in the bedroom before she could respond, and Paris found herself giggling when he tossed her unceremoniously onto one of the largest beds she'd ever seen. With her hands bound, there was little she could do to stop herself from bouncing into the air like an out-of-control pinball. "I have to say, I never would have imagined the joy I'd feel having my sub giggle during a scene, but damn if it isn't the sweetest thing I've ever heard."

Trinity surprised her when he leaned over to kiss the tip of her nose. The affectionate gesture warmed her heart. For a hard-ass cop, he could be surprisingly gentle, and she wondered how he got along with children. She'd assumed his towering height would frighten little ones, but now she considered how insightful most children were and believed they'd probably see right through his gruff exterior.

"I'm going to help you shut down that busy mind for a bit, Sprite. You have an interview later, and baby, you are wound way too tight. You need to relax, and I'm going to help you get there. I think four or five mind-melting orgasms ought to do it." Oh, Goddess in heaven, four or five of the soul-shattering releases she knew Trinity would give her would melt her bones. She'd be lucky to walk across the room, let alone down the long hall leading to the club. And she didn't even want to think about climbing those stone steps leading up to the third floor. Callie had told her the top level of the club held various offices, including Ian's and the conference room where she'd answer the FBI's questions.

Within seconds, Trinity had her hands secured above her and her legs bound with straps he pulled from under the edge of the over-sized mattress. He'd pushed pillows under her ass, raising it enough she was certain he'd be able to see her tonsils from his position at the end of the bed.

"You're not quite that open, Sprite. But I must say, the view is fucking spectacular. Your pussy is shiny with the sweetest nectar in the world, the lips already engorged with blood flowering in invitation. It's so easy to see why a woman's sex has been referred to as a blossoming rose— the resemblance is remarkable. Someday I'll take a picture so I can match the color—I'll send you dozens of the spectacular blooms, so you know how much I appreciate the sight."

Her ass was raised enough, Paris couldn't lift her head high enough to see him, but she could sense his every move. The first soft breath of air wafted over her clit, making her jerk against the restraints. "Easy, baby. I don't want you bruising those pretty wrists or ankles." Easy? Holy hell, he was lucky she hadn't launched herself right off the bed. His tongue snaked out to trace a circle around the pulsing bundle and Paris moaned. "Damn, I love hearing the sexy sounds you make when I play with you. Your body communicates what you love without you needing to say a word—although I do love the words, as well."

Another circle with the tip of his tongue, followed by a soft bite to the swollen bud sent her over the edge in a release she was entirely unprepared for. Pinpricks of light exploded behind her eyelids, the wonder of it sending her over the edge again as he soothed the small bite with gentle laps of his tongue.

"Two down, three to go. Open your eyes, baby. I want to be able to see the next one." Paris struggled to lift her heavy lids but finally managed to meet his gaze. Looking at her mate, his shoulders barely fitting between her upraised thighs, eyes darkened by desire, sent a fresh wash of cream leaking from her opening. Paris could feel the warm evidence of her need skimming her intimate flesh as his eyes never left hers. Watching his nostrils flare added to the volcanic look in his eyes. Damn the man could almost make her come from a look alone.

"I love your smooth pussy lips, baby. It makes you so sensitive and hides nothing from me. The deep blush of blood so close to the surface I can pick up traces of the coppery scent, it makes my cock so hard it feels like the damned thing may burst if I don't sink it into your heat. Go again for me baby, so we can get to the fun part." *The fun part? I think you missed the start of this party, Master.*

Any thoughts other than blinding pleasure were scattered in the explosion of sensation when Trin thrust two fingers deep inside, curving them forward until he pressed against the spongy spot deep inside sending her ass over teakettle into another release. Before she'd recovered enough to find her voice, he moved over her, thrusting so deep her swollen tissues burned so perfectly she fell over the edge again. Her mind was mush, but she heard him growl her name before his pounding thrusts sent her tumbling into a tunnel of brilliantly colored lights swirling all around her.

Struggling to catch her breath, Paris surfaced enough to feel Trinity's teeth scraping along the top of her shoulder. "Damn, you nearly pulled me over with you with the last one, Sprite. You tempt me in ways I never anticipated." His words were spoken in such a seductive tone, Paris found her body pulsing to life once again. *There's no way I can go again. My brain has already melted in a pile of goo.*

"Oh, but you can—and you will." Trinity canted his hips withdrew then slammed back into her tender channel. One thrust became a dozen, each one more devastating than the last until she was totally lost in the pleasure. His teeth clamped tight over the spot where he'd bitten her during their mating, launching her into an abyss of pure pleasure sweeter than Paris could have ever imagined existed. She heard a woman scream as Trinity shouted her name, but then the bright lights and colors receded until there was nothing but blissful silence.

Chapter Fifteen

PARIS LOOKED AROUND the spacious conference room, wishing she could turn around and walk right back out. *Holy shit! How many people did Ian McGregor invite to this little party?* Ian must have sensed her unease because she watched in resignation as he pushed away from the long mahogany table he'd been leaning against, his gaze set on her, his intent clear. Ian wasn't going to let her jettison back out the door—like the hulking man standing flush against her back was going to give her any avenue of escape.

"Oh, for heaven's sake, y'all are scaring her to death. I'll bet no one told her there was going to be a contingent waiting for her. I swear, Ian, you are just like my sons. Catherine warned me, but she's such a sweetie, I thought perhaps she was exaggerating."

Paris turned her attention to the woman weaving her way through the group. The older woman was stunningly beautiful, her dark hair cascading around a flawless face lit by the brightest blue eyes Paris had ever seen. Everyone in the room seemed frozen in place as the woman pulled her into a tight embrace.

"Hello, sugar. I'm Lilly West, and those two handsome

cowboys behind me are my husbands, Del and Dean. I'm Kent and Kyle West's mother, though there are days they would probably deny we're kin." She'd pulled back far enough to meet Paris' questioning gaze. The sincerity and warmth in Lilly's eyes let Paris relax enough to smile, though she doubted it reached her eyes. This woman was a mother to the depths of her soul. Paris recognized a spirit akin to her own mother's.

"That's it, sugar, you keep working on that smile until it's real. Fake it 'til ya make it is a thing, for sure. In the meantime, I want to introduce you to the best daughter any mama ever gained... I swear she is my heavenly reward for not strangling her men when they were kids." Where Lilly seemed surrounded by poise and grace, the petite blonde stepping forward was a bundle of barely restrained energy.

"Hi, I'm Tobi West. Those two gorgeous, growling men are mine, thanks to the wonderful matchmaking ability of their sweet mama. We planned a shopping trip and got shadowed, so you've inherited a couple of advocates and four more guardian angels." She'd said the last words with such saccharin sweetness, several people around them moaned. "I've met a few of your siblings, but I'm not allowed to tell you which ones or where." Tobi's eye-roll was an Oscar-worthy performance that made Paris giggle.

"Kitten." The more formidable looking of the two men who'd moved behind the spirited blonde growled her name. For just a second, Paris wondered if he was a shifter.

"He isn't." Trinity's warm breath washed over her ear, and Paris nodded her understanding. *Gotta remember about that link thing.*

"These fellas," Lilly gave an elegant wave around the room "give you any trouble, you just let me know, sugar. I might not have all their fancy Special Forces training, but I'm still the closest thing to a mama around here, and I'll use it for all it's worth."

"Don't we all know it?" The friendlier looking of Tobi's husbands stepped forward to introduce himself. Paris had read about Kent and Kyle West during her research of the lifestyle. Their reputations as sexual Dominants were as well-established as Ian McGregor's. It was easy to see why they were all friends.

"Thank you, ladies, for making Paris feel at home. I know it must have been intimidating walking into the room filled with folks you weren't expecting, but we wanted to have as many people here as possible, so we're all on the same page. This meeting is for information only. The agents who will interview Paris won't be on-site until tomorrow night." He noted her surprise and smiled. "We delayed them to give Israel and Catalina time to travel." She tipped her head in surprise—something in his tone told her there was more to the story.

"It would have alerted the men watching them if they'd both left New York to head to a kink club, baby. Trips to Club Isola are not usually family ventures." Trinity's explanation drew chuckles from several of the men around the room.

The group spent the next hour outlining everything they'd learned about her case, the pressure Senator Lamb was putting on the District Attorney in California to dismiss the charges, and her efforts to make Paris appear to be nothing more than a vengeful ex-girlfriend intent on destroying the good Senator's bid for re-election. By the time Paris heard everything the team had to say, she felt like her head was swimming. She must have looked as lost as she felt because warm hands covered the ice-cold ones on her lap, snapping her out of her moment of disconnection.

"Damn, girl, your hands are like ice." Abby's surprise was easy to hear in her voice, and Paris appreciated the easy friendship developing between them.

"Her hands are always cold, but ice might be something to worry about."

The sound of her older sister's voice had Paris on her feet before her mind fully registered it belonged to Catalina. How had she gotten so close without Paris realizing she was in the room? Launching herself into Cat's waiting embrace, Paris couldn't hold back a squeal of delight. Cat's arms closed around her, and Paris breathed a sigh of relief. It might be frustrating being the youngest in a large family, but there were perks too. While she knew Trinity would keep her safe, there was nothing like being wrapped in the warm hug of a sister.

"I'm so glad you're here." Paris hated hearing the need in her own voice, but she pushed the embarrassment aside.

"What am I, chopped liver?" Paris yelped when she was pulled from Cat's arms and pressed against Israel's muscular chest. "We're going to have a long chat about this, Imp. I don't like hearing about your struggles from someone else." The words of censure didn't hit her as hard as the disappointment she heard in his voice.

"I'm sorry, Is. I kept thinking I could handle it, then all

the sudden it was out of control."

"And you were too embarrassed to admit how far over your head you'd gotten?" Paris nodded; mortified things had spiraled out of control so quickly. Ian quickly outlined what they'd already covered, although it seemed Catalina and Israel both knew more than Paris had an hour ago.

People began filtering out of the room as Paris stood at the side watching. It amazed her so many people were working together to keep her safely out of David's and his mother's clutches. Watching Trinity from across the room, she marveled at how easily he worked with the other men and how intuitive he seemed when anticipating her needs. More than once, he'd appeared to sense her watching him and turned to meet her gaze. The first time, he'd summoned her to his side, checking to make sure she was hanging in there. After that, he'd simply winked, letting her know he was still nearby, and she was safe.

"He's a good man, Paris. I think you will be good for one another."

Turning, Paris met Cooper's gaze and smiled at the man she knew had fallen for her sister. Cooper Hicks and Catalina were both covert agents, their career paths crossing more often than most people realized. Watching the two of them dance around each other during London's wedding, Paris worried her sister was pushing Cooper aside. Now, she wondered if perhaps she'd misinterpreted Cat's interest because big sis sure seemed to be keeping the handsome former CIA agent in her line of sight.

"I'm not sure how good I'll be for Trinity. He's miles ahead of me in life experience. I'm not sure what I can bring to the table." It was the first time she'd expressed her fear out loud and hoped she hadn't said more than she should.

"You know, it's often easier to talk to someone you aren't emotionally connected to. It's not that I don't want us to become friends because the truth is, you remind me of my little sister, Lakyn. She's the best gift my parents ever gave me. Until she married, everything I did was with her best interest at heart. It was tough letting go, but she's in good hands."

"It sounds like your sister is very special." Watching his expression change as he spoke about his sister was heart-warming.

"She is. Lakyn loves huge." Paris tilted her head in question, making Cooper grin. "I'd always dreaded the time when Lakyn *replaced* me, but I'm coping."

"Oh, Cooper, I don't think any man can replace a brother. I have five of them, and they all bring something unique to my life. I've fallen in love with Trinity, but he doesn't replace anyone. I'd be diminishing his contribution to my life if I saw him that way." Paris felt Trinity's strong arms wrap around her from behind and relaxed back into this embrace.

"You're an amazing woman, Paris. I hope Trinity knows how lucky he is. I think you and Lakyn would be great friends. The last time I was home, I reminded her I'd always have her back, and essentially, she told me the same things you just mentioned—although you were much more diplomatic." Before turning to Trinity, Paris gave Cooper a quick hug.

"Lakyn is lucky to have such an amazing brother, I'm glad you are in Catalina's life." She saw him stiffen ever so slightly, but he didn't argue. Maybe he isn't as *in* as he'd like to be?

TRINITY STRUGGLED TO hold back the jealousy but wasn't sure how effective the effort was. He'd walked away in the middle of a conversation when he'd seen Paris talking to Cooper. *Fuck! I'm better than this, damn it.* He'd stood back for several seconds, listening to the exchange, proud as hell of the way his sweet mate handled the conversation. She'd displayed a remarkably mature sense of self, something he hadn't expected, considering her age and the fact she was the youngest in such a large family.

"I'm glad to hear you don't see me as a brother replacement, Sprite." Cooper chuckled as Trinity spoke from behind her.

"I'd be damned worried about your skill as a Dom if she did, Stone." Ian's teasing voice from beside her made Paris jump as Callie giggled.

"Master, you really shouldn't sneak up on subs. You are intimidating enough without adding a layer for a *pending ambush.*" Paris noted there was no censure in Callie's voice, she simply sounded as though she was looking out for the other submissives in the club. "You know your authority is unquestioned, Master, no need to startle a sub who is already being stalked by two people who are so... well, negligible." Paris burst out laughing, and Ian's grin told her he hadn't missed his wife's point.

"Well played, *Carlin*. Well played, indeed." Pulling her around in front of him, Ian ravaged her mouth in a kiss so hot, Trin looked down to see Paris fanning herself as her laughter subsided. When the club owner finally released his hold on his stunned wife, her eyes were glazed as she blinked, trying to bring his face back into focus, and her cheeks flushed a brilliant shade of scarlet. Paris watched as Ian kept both hands on her shoulders until he was certain she was steady before pulling her flush against his side. Thank heavens for great role models—Trinity could see Paris cataloging every nuance of Ian and Callie's encounter, pleased she had a chance to see others in the lifestyle.

"I plan to reward you, my clever little sub. I had something different planned, but I'm going to revise a bit. I think you'll appreciate the new direction, even more." After a quick nod to those around him, Ian led Callie away, making Paris wondered what the man had planned for her. *I hope it's not too intense, she seems so fragile.* Trinity chuckled beside her before leaning down to whisper in her ear.

"Baby, Callie McGregor is as tough as they come. She is also seventy-seven shades of smart and intuitive as any submissive I've ever met. Callie might not be as gifted as Mitch or Luke, but don't kid yourself, she reads people like a book."

Without missing a step, Callie cast an enchanting smile over her shoulder, proving Trinity had been right—Callie McGregor was anything but fragile. Paris found herself admiring the woman more with each encounter.

"Before Trinity whisks you away, I wanted to tell you we're having the pool party tomorrow afternoon. Tobi's making margaritas, and Lilly has charmed the chef at the resort kitchen into making snacks. I would have sworn that crotchety old coot who runs the kitchen couldn't be bought... but... shows you what I know. I swear that woman is my new hero." Trinity felt Paris shaking with laughter at Abby's nonsense, relieved she'd get some much-needed girl-time tomorrow.

The older he got, the more he understood the importance of friendship, and she was going to need the distraction after her morning interview with the FBI agents Ian was bringing in. The two were long-standing club members, and both were formidable—as law enforcement officers and Doms. They wouldn't settle for anything less than full disclosure. He hoped Paris didn't dig her heels in if things became too intense.

Stop pipe dreaming and take your curious mate for a walk through the club.

Chapter Sixteen

"**W**ALK WITH ME, Sprite." Trinity took Paris' hand, leading her into the club's main room. "We're going to have a look around, baby." Turning her, so she was facing him, Trin tipped her chin up so he could look into her sparkling blue eyes. Their considerable height difference was a constant challenge. He wished he'd stopped by the stairs—setting her on the second step made the disparity more manageable.

"The rules for tonight are very simple. You are not required to keep your eyes downcast—for the record, I will rarely require it. I want you to be a part of the activities, not visually excluded. But remember, looking does not mean touching or speaking. It's important you only speak when you are asked a direct question. If you have a question, squeeze my hand; that will let me know I need to stop so we can chat. Let's not give any of the newbie Doms a reason to think you should be under their lash, shall we?" When her eyes widened in fear, Trinity wanted to kick himself for being so blunt.

"I don't want anyone else to touch me. Maybe we should just leave. I'll watch how-to videos or something. Being quiet isn't my strong suit, anyway. If someone tries to put their hands on me, it's going to get ugly... really ugly, then I'll be in trouble with you and Ian. Holy cat balls, this is a very bad plan... terrible in fact. Come on, I'll make us a nice midnight snack, then we can surf porn sites. I promise to not set off any smoke detectors." *Great Goddess!* How had she managed all that without taking a damned breath? Cupping the sides of her face, he shook his head, kissing her forehead.

"Calm down, Sprite. I'm not letting anyone lay a hand on my mate. I was simply trying to avoid the confrontation I knew would follow." She'd gone white as a sheet, thinking another Dom might punish her. As much as he regretted scaring her, Trin still felt a small measure of satisfaction, knowing she was his and his alone.

"Take a deep breath, Paris." It seemed to take forever for this command to register, but she finally sucked in a breath. "Again." By the time she'd finished the second inhalation, the color was starting to return to her cheeks.

"SWEETNESS, YOU NEED to work on those breathing skills. It seems I always find you teetering on the cusp of collapsing into a heap. I'd hate to become another stalker, forced to follow you around to make sure you are all right." Kalen Black's sex-in-audible-form voice washed over her, soothing away the last of her frazzled nerves. If he ever found a way to market his voice, the man was going to leave Bill Gates in the dust.

"Thank you, Sir. I'll try to work on it. Thinking about any other Dom putting their hands on me is terrifying, and

I sort of launched into panic mode."

"I understand. As fiercely independent as our Tinker-bell Ninja is, she struggles with the same fear. Let me assure you, Ian has already carefully orchestrated your first club experience. You've quickly fallen under his umbrella of protection." Kalen's warm smile totally changed his appearance, seeming to light him up from the inside. Paris hoped Abby knew how blessed she was.

Paris had been confused by Kalen's comment about Ian orchestrating her experience, but it didn't take her long to figure it out. The men surrounding them changed effortlessly—even after she realized what was happening, she had trouble keeping track of the seamless transitions. Whoever choreographed the changes was a genius. *No shit, Sherlock. Everyone knows Ian McGregor is a genius. Damn, I really need to get out more.*

"Be careful, baby, you are getting close to the edge. I won't allow you to belittle yourself. I won't allow anyone to speak negatively about my greatest treasure."

Damn, he could melt her with just a few words. *I really am too easy. Yep, need to get out more, for sure.*

DAVID LAMB STOOD on the yacht's deck, watching the trees he'd been told shielded the entrance to Club Isola. What the hell was Paris doing in a fucking sex club? She didn't belong in a place catering to perverts. How the hell was he supposed to erase this from her past? Fucking hell, his mother was going to have a damned coronary when she got wind of this. Maybe with a little luck, he'd be able to keep Paris' location a secret long enough to get her off the damned island tomorrow. He planned to anchor offshore tonight. The security detail he'd hired were having a grand time partying—they'd easily gotten fully into their cover as a group of drunken guys out fishing and enjoying some R & R.

The Harbor Master had been helpful—for a price—explaining the club would ferry guests to and from the island until approximately two in the afternoon. After that, there would be almost no boat traffic around the small patch of land. David planned to use the small onboard launch to get to the shore, hiding the small craft in a small copse of trees or under the dock. He'd move up the path, grab Paris, and get her the hell out of whatever mess she'd gotten herself into.

The syringe in his pocket was filled with a sedative designed to make the recipient compliant and manageable while leaving them able to walk under their own power. Paris wasn't a large woman, but he wasn't sure he'd be able to carry her down the rocky shore, so this was his best hope to get her out of the public relations nightmare she'd landed in. Not to mention, it would cloud any questions about kidnapping—at least until she came to her senses and married him.

Paris belonged to him. She always had. Damn it, she was just confused. They'd fly to the resort he'd booked in Fiji, spend some time alone, and she'd see how perfect they were together. Hell, they'd been best friends for years, and he'd been in love with her from the moment they met. She loved him, too—he knew she did. He'd gotten desperate when she wouldn't stop talking about that damned Sheriff and overplayed his hand.

Resting his high-power binoculars on the rail of the luxury yacht, David shook his head. He needed to be careful. He couldn't afford to make another mistake. Hell, his mother was already going thermonuclear, any other smear on her reputation would likely send her into orbit or worse. The good Senator was a ruthless bitch when crossed. David usually did everything he could to stay just inside her peripheral view. He'd learned years ago—distance was his friend when dealing with his mother.

Unfortunately, his arrest for the *Paris incident*, as his mother referred to it, landed him front and center on not only her radar but the media's as well. So far, his mother's public relations team had done a great job keeping a lid on it, but that wouldn't last forever. The only thing that kept him from having to deal with the Adlers was the redaction of Paris' name from the press release. David wasn't naïve enough to believe it was anything more than a temporary reprieve. The addition of Luke Grayson to the Adler family was a real pain in David's ass. So far, he'd managed to stay one step ahead of the famed computer expert, but the bastard would get lucky at some point and stumble on the information.

Heading back inside the yacht's luxurious cabin, David grabbed one of the gourmet submarine sandwiches the onboard chef had left in the refrigerator for their late night snacking, tucked a couple of bottles of beer in the pockets of his board shorts, and headed to the rooftop deck with his iPad. It hadn't taken him long to find pictures of the small island's new resort, but photos of the club were nowhere to be found. Fucking unbelievable there hadn't been a security breach in all the years the club had been in operation.

Hell, even the satellite images of the island weren't much help. He'd magnified the damned images into oblivion, but the aerial view was so shrouded by landscaping, you could only catch fleeting glimpses of the walking paths connecting the McGregor's home, resort, and club. Ian McGregor might be a secretive bastard, but he was no fool.

If the rumors were true, the club was built in a natural cave. Since the interior would still be vulnerable to fire, he knew there were multiple exits. David's goal was to find the main service entrance—it would have the most traffic, making it easier for him to blend in. Studying the SAT images, he finally zeroed in on what looked like a dock on the Atlantic side. After several minutes spent enlarging and enhancing the picture, he was able to make out a dolly cart and what appeared to be a golf cart on steroids. *Bingo!*

"HE HAS TO be the dumbest fucker on the planet." Jace watched the aerial footage from the drone circling the yacht anchored offshore. The Coast Guard had confirmed the well-appointed vessel was a rental, and a quick call to the owner revealed the man who'd signed the contract used a fake name. Jace's team spoke with the agency's front desk clerk, who'd identified David Lamb as one of the occupants.

"I know the drone is high, and it's virtually silent, but damn, don't people ever look up?"

"Not usually. Why do you think Spiderman could hide by clinging to the ceiling?" Abby's voice sounded from beside him, and Jace turned to his sister, shaking his head.

"Spiderman? Really, Tink? I thought you outgrew that movie after the seven hundred and thirty-second viewing." After one particularly torturous leave spent at home, Jace had told his parents he wasn't coming back again until they'd burned her recording of that damned movie. He'd seen it so many times, he'd was able to recite the dialogue, word for fucking word.

His mom and dads hadn't been terribly sympathetic since they were stuck watching it whenever he and his buddies were away, but they'd promised to get rid of the tape before his next break, and they had. She'd exacted her revenge by recording some damned show with a purple dinosaur named Barney over all the porn tapes he hadn't hidden well enough. Damn, she'd been a pain in his ass and was still the best gift his parents had ever given him. He'd fallen in love with the red-faced, squalling bundle the minute they'd walked through the door with her.

"Where are your, men? I thought you were playing tonight, that's why I'm working outside security." That and the fact the pride of the *Participation Trophy Generation* was anchored off the coast, researching how to make his way ashore. Jace had seen the results of spoiled brats his entire life, but this joker was ranking at the top of the heap. When Abby sagged into a chair, heaving a huge sigh, Jace studied her with a critical eye. She looked tired, and that was out of character—the complete antithesis of the young woman who was usually a fucking Energizer bunny.

"They were tag-teaming with security for Paris. Believe

it or not, there was a hiccup in the great and powerful Ian's plan, so I begged off and promised I'd find you."

So, her men had been willing to let her leave but wanted her in his care. *Interesting.* His wife, Holly, had tried to convince him a few weeks ago he was going to be an uncle, but he'd blown off her observation as wishful thinking. His woman was more than ready to be an aunt, and since she was an only child, Abby was her only hope.

"What's up, Tink? Talk to me, sweetheart." Her eyes filled with tears, and he barely had time to open his arms before she launched herself out of her chair and into his waiting embrace, clinging to him like a damned spider monkey. Jace was so stunned, it took him a few seconds to figure out his little sister was drowning in a hormonal soup. Hell, Holly cried when watching commercials on television while she was pregnant. He'd finally banned all television and social media, but it had been wasted effort because she'd started reading romance novels and promptly gone right back over the edge.

"I'm going to be the worst mother in the history of mothers. And Mama is going to be so mad." *Mad? Is she kidding?* Their parents were going to be over the moon.

"Why on earth would she be angry, Tink? Hell, she's been pestering you three since the day of your wedding for this news." Jace was baffled. It was out of character for his sister to be wrong about anything, but she was certainly off the mark this time.

"I'm five months along. We didn't want to tell anyone because I've had two miscarriages. I didn't want to get anybody's hopes up."

"And now you think you've waited too long? That

Mom and the Dads will be angry because they didn't know sooner?" He felt her stiffen in his arms and knew she'd heard how absurd it sounded. "Sometimes, you need to say things out loud, Tink. When you bounce a worry off someone else, and it comes back sounding crazy, you have a choice. You can continue worrying needlessly, or you can accept it's not reasonable and move on."

Abby hiccupped as he set her gently on her feet. Jace knew she hadn't seen Logan and Kalen come into the room, and he was grateful they were giving him a chance to, once again, be the big brother she'd always come to with her heartaches. He didn't get the opportunity to fill that role very often these days.

"It doesn't sound right when you say it, but in my head, it was a big deal. I don't understand what's happening, it's like my brain keeps short-circuiting. The book says it's called... Cra... fish, I can't ever remember what they called not being able to remember anything. Where's Holly? She'll remember. Holy rickrack. What if I forget where I left the baby after she's born?"

She? I'm getting a niece?

Abby was a genius by anyone's measure, but he'd learned a long time ago, intelligence couldn't always make its way to the surface when a woman was drowning in pregnancy hormones. He'd seen it with Callie and Holly. Adding to the mix was the strain of keeping a secret he knew she had to be dying to share, and it was a recipe for a meltdown of Biblical proportions.

"Abby, call Mom. She's going to be over the moon, I promise. Of course, the Dads are going to send the company jet for you, but you look like you could use some mothering. And just for the record—you're going to be an amazing mother. Hell, you're the best aunt in the world, and you've got two amazing husbands to help." Smoothing her hair back from her face, Jace grinned when she sighed. Pressing a kiss against her forehead, he assured her, "You're going to be fine, and I promise to smuggle root beer into the hospital for you." Her smile lit up the room. He'd always smuggled root beer to her when she'd been sick. His mention of it now filled her eyes with unshed tears, but they were happy tears, and those didn't shred his heart.

Abby needed to call their parents as soon as possible—not because they needed to hear the news, but because she wasn't going to be able to relax and enjoy the experience until she'd shared the news.

Damn, I'm going to be an uncle! And my wife is never going to let me forget she was right.

Chapter Se enteen

PARIS WASN'T SURE where Abby had gone, and now, both Kalen and Logan were missing as well. She'd been told Abby's brother, Jace, was working outer security because he didn't want to be in the club while his younger sister was inside. Since Abby had seemed to have vanished into thin air, Paris wondered if she'd get to finally meet the infamous Jace Garrett.

"Doubtful, Beautiful. Gage and Holly are in their private lair here at the club. I'm sure Jace is anxious to join them." She respected Jace's decision to not be in the club when his sister was there, Paris didn't have any desire to watch any of her siblings play in a club either. *Gross!* "I'm a bit of an exhibitionist, sweetness, but I'll draw the line at doing scenes in front of your family."

Holy hairballs… she didn't even want to think about having sex in front of her family. *Disgusting.* She felt Trinity shaking with laughter beside her, but decided it wasn't worth the argument to tell him all the reasons she thought he was an ass. She realized her mistake as soon as the thought floated through her mind, but it was too late.

"You don't have to tell me, baby. I already know what you're thinking. Damn, this is about the handiest gift the

Great Goddess has ever given me."

Paris had no response, she was too stunned to respond. Did he mean his ability to hear her thoughts was the gift— or was she the gift? When she heard his exasperated sigh, she realized her mind had drifted once again.

"Your mind is a complicated maze I'd never be able to navigate without the extra help. I have no idea how men make relationships work without this advantage."

She didn't miss the note of amusement in his tone. *Don't worry, Sprite. I suspect our telepathic link is already building. Soon you'll be able to hear me, and your connection to the others in our pack will follow.* Paris was stunned. Completely blindsided by what had just occurred. Spinning around to face him, she realized too late how close they were and tumbled backward when she tried to meet his gaze.

Paris felt herself falling, her arms flailing wildly in mid-air. Trying to reach for Trinity's outstretched hand, she inadvertently arched her back which sent the back of her skull on a collision course with the stone floor. An explosion of pain made her stomach roll a split second before she descended into darkness.

TRINITY TRIED DESPERATELY to get his hands on Paris as her arms pinwheeled wildly in front of her. By the time she locked her gaze on his outstretched hand, she was too close to the floor. Arching in a desperate attempt to grasp his hand sent the back of her head crashing against the floor. If he lived another century, Trinity knew he'd never forget the sound or the overwhelming helplessness he'd felt at that moment.

Teetering between the place where his training as a cop and first responder would ordinarily kick in and pure panic as Paris' mate, Trinity felt frozen in mid-animation for an eternity. Truthfully, it could have only been fractions of a second, but when time stands still, it's damned hard to judge.

Members and staff immediately surrounded them, including Jace Garrett, who seemed to appear from thin air, radio in hand, barking orders. In the cacophony of sound, the only word Trinity caught was *chopper*. Ian and Callie made their way to his side, Ian gathering information from those gathered around, those who'd seen Paris fall provided as much detail as they could.

Callie laced her warm fingers with his much cooler ones, the small gesture of friendship and support, sending a flood of warmth through him. Trinity smiled down at the owner's lovely wife and nodded. Damn, he owed her. With a simple show of unconditional support, she'd pulled his head out of his ass.

"Thank you, Callie. I'm okay now." Taking a deep breath, Trinity pushed his training to the forefront as the club's medics began covering the gash on the back of Paris' head and strapped her to a backboard.

Trinity helped carry her out to the waiting helicopter, uncertain where they were headed but confident Ian and Jace were making sure his sweet mate was going to get the best care available. Behind them, he heard Catalina yelling at someone to let her go as Cooper Hick's deep voice calmly explained why he wouldn't allow her to jeopardize her sister's safety by delaying medical treatment. As reasonable as Cooper's explanation was, the words were falling on deaf ears.

We'll be right behind you. Ian has people waiting on the roof of George Washington. Israel's voice moved through his mind with such fluid ease, Trinity was startled—though he shouldn't have been. When they were in their wolf form, telepathic communication often made the difference between life and death, so it was an evolutionary skill, finely honed over several millennia.

I'll leave everything but Paris to you. She is my sole focus. Trinity would let Israel and Catalina contact the rest of their family, although he'd bet his last nickel Luke Grayson was already on it. When he'd first joined Club Isola, Trinity had been impressed with Ian McGregor's extensive network of resources, but he'd never been as grateful for the man's tireless dedication to the safety of his members until this moment. Knowing he kept a medi-vac helicopter and medical staff on site could easily make the difference between life and death in the event of a traumatic injury.

The flight only lasted a few short minutes—a fraction of the time it would have taken if they' been forced to take the ferry and drive to the hospital. Paris had begun stirring as the chopper lifted off and was fully awake, though visibly confused by the time they landed. He'd held her hand during the flight, and the only time she offered any resistance to being transported was when he'd been forced to release his hold during the unloading process.

"No. Don't leave me. Why is it so dark here?" *Dark?* Hell, the rooftop was lit up like a fucking Christmas tree.

"I'm not leaving you, baby." In seconds, he had her

hand back in his, and they were sprinting to where several men and women in white lab coats stood waiting. After a flurry of questions and answers, they moved inside. The next two hours were filled with so many tests, Trinity finally started making a list, just to keep track. The waiting room was full to the point of bursting, and he was grateful Israel was handling everything not related directly to his mate's care.

Trinity wasn't sure what story Ian had given the staff, but no one questioned his relationship with Paris or his right to make decisions about her care. He wasn't sure whether to be impressed by the man's influence or concerned it was so effective. Thank Goddess, the cut on the back of Paris' scalp was small enough, it only required a few stitches, and they hadn't cut her hair. Hell, the only time he'd seen Paris cry during the whole ordeal was when one of the nurses announced they'd be shaving a six-inch diameter circle at the back of her head as she set out scissors and a razor. Paris had burst into tears, and it had taken every ounce of control Trinity possessed to keep from ripping the woman, limb from limb.

The doctor had walked in, quickly assessing the situation, shaken his head in disgust, and pushed the tray aside. He'd given Paris a gentle smile and assured her he had no need to even trim her pretty, long locks.

Trinity recognized the nurse as a sub who'd attended a club as a visitor a few times, but he'd never seen her there on her own, so she either couldn't swing the expensive membership fee or hadn't made it through Ian's rigorous screening. Judging by the way she'd intentionally upset Paris, Trinity was betting on the latter. He made a mental note to mention her behavior to Ian. *Your lack of compassion won't go unpunished little sub.* Ian would see to it she never set foot in his club again. The woman's behavior had been unacceptable on multiple levels.

The neurological team asked to meet with Trinity, Israel, and Catalina. When he asked who she wanted to sit with her, Paris surprised him by asking for Lilly West. Kent and Kyle had chuckled when he asked if she would mind. Lilly shot them a searing glare.

"Every girl wants a mama when she's feeling punk. You two are clueless." Lifting her chin in the air like the supermodel she'd once been, Lilly West strode down the hall to Paris' room as everyone in the room stared in awe.

"You two never learn, do you?" Dean West shook his head, looking on as his sons mirrored baffled expressions.

"They never did understand their mama. You boys would do well to figure this out because your children spend a lot of time with their Grammy. Don't think for a minute she isn't having an impact. If you can't handle our sweet wife, your daughter is going to hand your ass to you on a silver platter." The room erupted into laughter, and Trinity felt like he'd just taken his first deep breath in several hours.

Listening to the doctors describe the symptoms and treatments of a closed brain injury left him reeling. He'd noticed Paris had asked the same question several times, but he'd been pulled out to sign papers so often, Trinity hadn't realized how severe her concussion was.

"What about her eyesight? She mentioned how dim the lights seemed when we landed, and the entire roof looked like it was high noon."

"It isn't uncommon. Paris hit the back of her head, specifically the occipital lobe, the part of the brain responsible for processing visual information. We're monitoring the swelling, but she's already responding to treatment, so I don't expect any long-term problems. It's important she does not drive for a few weeks, and it might be several months before she is comfortable driving at night. Ideally, she'd recover somewhere she could use golf carts to get around. Perhaps a nice resort?"

Trinity, Catalina, and Israel all smiled. They had the perfect place, there was even a nice fence to keep the little rebel corralled. The tunnel was well lit, so she could go see London any time of the day or night. It was the perfect solution. They just needed to get her there.

LILLY CROSSED THE room, promptly pulling Paris into a gentle hug, unsurprised when the young woman dissolved into tears.

"Damn, girl, you've had one hell of a night. You let all those tears wash away every bit of the negative nonsense you've had to deal with. From what I hear, you are very lucky, though I doubt it feels that way right now." Paris needed to decompress, and there was nowhere better for a young woman to do that than the loving arms of a mother.

Lilly was honored Paris had asked for her and hoped they'd be able to develop a close relationship, despite the obvious challenges the distance between them would pose. Paris needed a mother and Lilly needed to be needed... they were perfect for one another. Smiling as she felt Paris relax, Lilly patted her back and helped her sit back up.

"You close those eyes for a few, sugar. I'm going to get you a cool compress. We'll get that swelling down in no time. Trinity comes in here and sees you've been cryin', he'll scold me. Hell, I don't need another man barkin' up my tree. My husbands are the best thing since sliced bread, but they're a bossy pair, don't you think for a minute they aren't. And those sons of mine think they're all that and a bag of chips." Pouring the ice water from a small pitcher into the sink basin, Lilly soaked a washcloth, then laid it gently over Paris' eyes and upper cheeks.

"You know, I was a model when I met my men. Everybody thinks I gave up this fabulous career to marry two men, but what most people didn't realize was my career wasn't anything I was particularly proud of. I knew I was supposed to feel short-changed, hell, I was a part of the generation who burned their bras and fought for equal pay. We started the feminist movement... no offense, but your generation is being lied to about what feminism is about." She heard Paris' soft giggle and smiled to herself. *Perfect.*

"Anyway, I'll bet your mama had her hands full with ten kids. Lordy, I can barely wrap my head around it. My boys were enough to make me take up drinkin', I'd have probably drowned myself in margaritas with ten kids. Being the youngest, I bet you have some great stories. Everybody always forgets the youngest kids are in the room." Paris pulled the cloth from her face, staring at Lilly with something between wonder and amusement.

"How could I have forgotten? You're right, everyone spoke freely because they didn't think I was old enough to understand what they were talking about. I learned a lot that way." Lilly saw her bright blue eyes begin to spark to life and breathed a sigh of relief. The storm had passed, and Paris might end up gaining a bit of valuable perspective from their little chat.

"I'll make you a deal. You get all healed up, and we'll plan a big, girls' trip into the city for a few days. There's nothing like New York City during the holidays, and it drives Kent and Kyle crazy when I take Tobi out from under their watchful eyes for a few days." Waving her hand as if dismissing the notion, Lilly grinned. "I work hard to be a pain in their asses for a couple of reasons.

"First, they have it coming... in spades, honey. Those two were wild as the Texas wind and just as damned unpredictable... then they decided to become Navy SEALs, and proud as I was of them, for years, every time the phone rang, my heart skipped a beat. I also feel pestering those two helps Tobi out a bit as well, and I couldn't love that girl more if I'd given birth to her. If her men are worrying about what sort of nonsense I'm dreaming up, they tend to give her a bit more freedom because they see how good she is compared to me." Lilly gave Paris a triumphant smile when she laughed but felt a pang of guilt when she winced, cradling her hands on both sides of her head as if trying to keep it from blowing apart.

"Damn, I'm sorry, sweetie. I'll try to tone down my sparkling personality a bit, so you don't end up with a headache worse than I suspect is already barreling down on you." Soaking the cloth in the ice bath again, Lilly rolled it and laid it gently over her eyes. "You just sit back and tell me one of your favorite stories about your mama." She'd no sooner spoken the words than the door opened. When

Catalina led the others into the room, Lilly held her finger to her lips. The three of them nodded their assent despite the questions she could see in their eyes.

"I remember sitting in the tree outside our kitchen window one spring afternoon when I was probably four or five. The older kids had gotten into some kind of dust-up at school, and our parents weren't happy with them. Dad was lecturing them on all the reasons violence isn't the answer, but even at that age, I knew his argument wasn't cutting it. My brothers and sisters had come to the defense of the little girl who lived down the street. Her dad had committed suicide when he was caught stealing from the bank where he worked, and some of the kids in her class were making fun of her."

"Oh, sugar, I can only imagine what was going through your young mind." Lilly held her hand over her heart as she listened to Paris' heart-wrenching story.

"It wasn't as bad as you think because it was the first time I can remember thinking my dad was wrong and knowing you can be wrong for all the right reasons." Lilly watched as Paris rolled the rag from one side to the other without opening her eyes and breathed a sigh of relief; she still didn't know she had an audience. Paris' depth of understanding at four years old was remarkable and proved everything she'd hear about the newly graduated educator's recent job interview hadn't been overstated.

"Dad thought the older kids should have gone to an adult, but they'd insisted there wasn't enough time. There was a lot of back-and-forth discussion, but it was Mom's argument I remember. She said they'd taught the girl to be defenseless. I didn't know what that meant, at least not entirely, but I understood her explanation."

PARIS WOULD NEVER forget hearing her mother's soft voice waft through the open window.

"You won't always be there to help her, just as your father and I won't always be here to help you. That's why we try to teach you how to deal with life's challenges. We want to know you can defend yourself... and that you'll help others become empowered as well. Would you rather your father beat up someone hurting one of you? How would that help you tomorrow or next week when the bullies return? If you want to help Melissa and her mother, help the little girl learn how to defend herself. Help her find ways to channel her frustration. Take the time to make sure she knows you believe in her... there's no greater gift."

The silence that followed her mother's impassioned words had been louder than anything Paris had ever heard. She remembered lying in the tree for a long time, staring up at the twinkling stars and wondering if she'd ever be as smart as her mama. Hopefully, by the time she was a mother, she'd be as wise as the woman who'd been taken from them far too soon.

"After my brothers and sisters were sent upstairs to bed, my parents sat at the kitchen table, talking about how they were going to help Melissa's mama. We didn't have a lot of money, but somehow, my mom and dad got enough together to help them move at the end of school. Melissa never came back to our school, but I've thought of her often. Before they moved, my brothers and sisters taught her how to defend herself. But most of all, they were just her friends, and I think that's what made the most difference. I've often wondered what happened to her."

When she pulled the cloth from her face, Paris was surprised to find Israel typing silently on the screen of his phone as Catalina stood beside him, huge tears streaking down her flushed cheeks. But it was Trinity who captured her attention. The look of love and admiration in his eyes made her heart stutter.

"That's a beautiful story, baby. You should write down all those sweet memories. They'd make a wonderful gift to our children."

Without thinking, Paris tried to get out of bed. The only thing she wanted was to be in his arms. She hadn't realized how many things the doctors had attached to her, and the alarms blared as the leads popped off. "Stop!" Trinity's one-word command made her freeze, giving him time to take the few steps separating them. He'd no more than pulled her against his chest than the door slammed open, a steady stream of medical personnel filling the room.

The nurse who'd threatened to cut her hair gave Paris a scathing look, and Trinity growled deep in his chest, the vibration soothing Paris and terrifying Nurse Ratched. There was a strange crackling in the air between Trinity and Israel before her brother turned on the woman.

"You. Come with me." He grasped her elbow, escorting her out the door, leaving Catalina and Lilly blinking in confusion.

"I told you letting her come back here alone was dangerous." Paris turned her attention to the door and smiled at the indulgent looks the handsome faces of Del and Dean West.

"It boggles the mind how she manages to land in the middle of pandemonium, looking fresh as a daisy and as gorgeous as the day we met her."

Damn, Lilly's men brought back memories of her own father. He'd been tall with broad shoulders narrowing to slender hips. Before he'd died, her dad's hair had been graying at the temples, and she'd thought he was the most handsome man in the world when he'd laughingly called the change *wisdom highlights*.

"Damn, girl. I thought somebody started a pinball tournament back here. Lights flashing, bells ringing, and beepers blaring. It was frick-fracking exciting until my brain turned back on. Holy cat balls, how's your head?"

Paris blinked as she looked around her. Things were still dim, but for the first time since all the drama in California, Paris felt herself relax, confident everything was going to be fine.

A year was a long time to live under the strain Paris had been subjected to. She'd wondered if she'd ever be able to trust enough to have friends again, and now, she found herself surrounded by a group of people who'd offered their support and friendship without asking for anything in return. They weren't trying to score an introduction to one of her siblings, they weren't trying to form a political alliance by marrying one of the owners of Adler Oil. The only reason David's mother had tolerated Paris as her son's friend was her desire to align herself with Austin, and the good senator had obviously known more about her son's interest than Paris had.

"Come on everybody, let's invade the cafeteria. It's always fun to see the panic on their faces when a large group of Texans walk in." Turning back to Paris, Lilly winked. "I'm looking forward to our girls' trip, sugar. We're going to scheme up something spectacular."

A collective moan sounded from the men as the women snickered. The room might still be cast in subtle shadows, but Paris suddenly realized how bright her future looked.

Chapter Eighteen

"**I**'M CONVINCED HE is the dumbest son of a bitch on the planet." Jace Garrett stood with his booted feet spread shoulder length apart, arms crossed over his muscled chest, staring at the wall-mounted monitor in Ian's office.

"The hospital staff has been circulating the story one of our resort guests fell breaking a hip. The last I heard, there had been two different inquiries they suspected were from Senator Lamb's camp. It seems her son likes to use his mother's staff as his personal assistants when it suits him."

"Not surprised. I can't imagine the little fucker plans to do much with his life aside from living off the millions his mother has mysteriously acquired as a government employee." Jace had no use for crooked politicians, and it seemed the club's staff was always dealing with them in one capacity or another. *Hell, I need a fucking vacation.*

"I assume your greeting committee is in place." Jace laughed because Ian's question was a contender for understatement of the week.

"We had more volunteers than I had places for them. With Paris on her way back to Massachusetts, I have mixed feelings about scooping the little bastard up." Turning his focus to Ian, he knew his friend understood the dilemma. Local law enforcement wouldn't be able to charge Lamb with anything other than unlawful entry. Hell, he'd be out of the local lockup in an hour. The only way they'd catch a break would be if he were stupid enough to bring some sort of drawn plan, but since there were no schematics of the island available, he'd have to have drawn them himself from satellite images. *Dimwit probably doesn't know which end of a crayon to use.*

"I understand and agree. The FBI agents who interviewed Paris before she was discharged were impressed with her ability to recall details despite her head injury."

"From what I heard, they cautioned her it probably wouldn't be enough to convince the D.A. to take the case to trial, which is damned frustrating." Jace hated knowing David Lamb was going to get away with stalking and sexual assault. He was also concerned Paris was just getting a temporary reprieve. Men like Lamb didn't stop until they were forced to.

"The D.A. isn't going to risk pissing off a powerful politician, known for being vengeful, to prosecute a case he doesn't think he can win. It's sad but true—prosecutors are worried about their success ratio and their future political aspirations." Jace knew Ian was right, but that didn't stop it from grating on his last nerve.

"I'm not making any promises about his condition when the locals get their hands on him." Jace knew his grin probably made him look like a deranged crackpot, but he didn't care. David Lamb was going to get his ass handed to him as soon as he stepped foot on shore. Ian chuckled as he zoomed in on the man, struggling to row the small boat the last hundred yards. Lamb killed the motor a quarter mile out, no doubt under the mistaken impression he wouldn't be noticed if his entry was silent.

"I'd expect nothing less. If his resistance doesn't look convincing enough, we'll suffer some mysterious recording glitch." Ian's negligent shrug was almost amusing. "It happens."

Not in Jace's system it didn't, but he could damned well play that card if he needed to.

GAGE LEANED AGAINST a large tree, watching David Lamb struggle to row ashore. Jesus, Joseph, and Mary, today was one of the calmest days Jace had ever seen on the Atlantic side of the island, and the pansy-ass was probably going to have a damned heart attack before he managed to get the small dingy close enough to pull it ashore. Hell, Callie had rowed a small boat across the bay in rougher seas and in the damned dark. *Fucking pussy.*

"You'd better be talking about that candy ass and not me, my friend." Tony Dent nodded his head in David Lamb's direction, his low-pitched voice doing little to hide his Italian heritage. Jace knew the other man's teammates had often teased him about sounding like a character in *The Godfather* and smiled to himself. Tony joined McGregor Holdings security team after losing a portion of one leg while serving in the Navy SEALs. The injury hadn't slowed him down, but the desk job Uncle Sam offered hadn't held any appeal.

Gage admired Tony's calm demeanor but hated the

pain he'd seen in the other man's eyes when subs rejected him based solely on what he'd lost. Jace and Ian both regularly shut down efforts by Callie and Holly to play matchmaker, but Gage wasn't foolish enough to believe the two hadn't enlisted the help of his wife's best friend and Jace's younger, wild-child sister. If Abby was involved, the whole thing could go up like the fucking Fourth of July. He only hoped the three of them didn't drive Tony away from Club Isola with their damned machinations.

"I'm never getting close enough to your happy ass to find out what it's made of, Tony. But just for the record, I was talking about the limp-armed mama's boy trying to row ashore. Hell, we may have to send Callie out to show him how it's done." Tony snorted a laugh, shaking his head in disgust.

"Is the little fucker armed?"

"Yes. A decent sized knife in one boot and a small caliber handgun in the other. I still can't believe the asshat never looked up. If I planned to kidnap a woman off Ian McGregor's private island, I'd fucking be looking around me like a wild man." Personally, Gage agreed with Jace and Ian. David Lamb was dangerous for several reasons—his access to quick money, the protection of a crooked politician, and balls bigger than his damned brain. "The weapons aren't as big a concern as the damned syringe Jace saw him tuck in his shirt pocket. Get it. They aren't going to be able to make much of a case here, so preserving evidence isn't a concern, but we damned well want to know what he planned to use."

The team would relay the information to Trinity in case Lamb decided to make another play for Paris. The plan was to make a huge public spectacle of today's incident and hope his mother yanked him back in line.

"I still can't believe you're letting Abby in on this. Hell, I'd have thought you would have intervened even if her brother allowed it."

"We choose our battles carefully with Abby. She's pregnant, not helpless, and we've learned from experience, she is safer when we keep her in plain sight. It's when she decides to fly under our radar, we have issues." Abby and Paris resembled one another enough to make them easy to confuse from a distance. The goal was for Lamb to spot a woman he believed was his target and walk directly into their trap. They needed him far enough inland to negate any argument he was nothing more than a stranded boater.

Gage watched as Lamb struggled to pull the small craft far enough onto the rocks under the service dock, evidently, the nearby trees would be too much trouble. *What a lazy ass.* He didn't bother looking around for cameras, which probably shouldn't surprise anyone since he'd just spent most of the weekend with a drone hovering overhead without noticing.

"Who's covering?" Gage knew exactly what Tony was asking. They never left anything to chance, and with Abby set to appear at the top of the trail, this wasn't a time to let their guard down.

"Logan is in the crow's nest behind the club; he'll have the clearest shot to defend Abby. Lilly West is on a third-floor balcony at the resort." The angle would keep Lilly from shooting in Logan's direction, and the goal was to keep her from shooting at all. Although she was a crack shot, she was also known for being a wild card. Hopefully, with her husbands flanking her, they wouldn't have any surprises. Tony chuckled, shaking his head. Gage saw him glance toward the resort.

"Damn, that woman is a firecracker. The Wests' team was my second choice when I knew it was time to leave the SEALs. I'd met her once several years earlier, and she was almost enough to make me move to Texas." Gage hadn't known the Wests contacted Tony but wasn't surprised. "My sister begged me to stay close. She swore she needed the help since her husband travels a lot. I know caring for two small kids was a lot to handle on her own, but I can count on one hand the number of times she's needed my help."

"Let me guess, the number of times she's needed to check on you is much higher?"

"Yes, indeed. She played me like a damned song."

"Well, I'm glad. And I know Ian and Jace would say the same." It was true, Tony was an integral part of the team. "Looks like muscle-man is finally on the move. Let's get this show on the road." Tapping the mic on his comm unit, Gage updated the rest of the team.

Showtime.

ABBY BOUNCED ON the balls of her feet, anxious to get this done. The energy coursing through her needed an outlet, and kicking David Lamb a few times would go a long way to letting off some of the steam. She hadn't been able to spar in months and knew it would be several more before she was allowed any full body contact. Getting in a few jabs and kicks was going to be therapeutic. *Damn, I hope he isn't going to be all sweet and sappy. I swear I'll ralph on his damned shoes.*

The earbud she'd been given crackled to life, her brother's southern drawl filled her ear. "Settle down, Tink. Your heart rate is spiking. I'll pull your ass out if you don't chill."

"You'd have to catch me first, Indy." As a kid, she'd been a huge Indiana Jones fan, and since her big brother was her hero, the nickname had seemed only natural. "This one is for Paris. I wish she could take him out herself, but this is the next best thing."

Ian had arranged for Trinity and Paris to be flown back home. The doctors had only agreed to release her because they'd been completely dumbfounded by her rapid recovery. Of course, having a well-known physician living onsite had also been a huge part of the decision.

Dr. Evan Monroe's reputation was impeccable. Not only was he an incredibly skilled surgeon, but the security of his facility made it a favorite for anyone with enough money and a strong desire to keep their stay private. Evan originally designed the secure facility to keep his work with shifters from the prying eyes of public hospital employees, but it quickly became known as the place to go for the rich and secretive.

"You have to come home eventually, little sister, and I'm a patient man."

"Since when."

"Since the day Mom and Dad walked in with you." Abby couldn't hold back her giggle because she knew it was true. He'd been the most patient big brother a girl could have ever asked for. She'd given him trouble at every turn, but she also loved him with everything she had. Her brother was an amazing father and would be the best uncle on the planet.

Out of her peripheral vision, Abby saw David Lamb approaching. He was moving at a good clip, obviously hoping to sneak up on her.

"Lamb has a syringe in his front shirt pocket, Tink. Do not, under any circumstance, let him near you with that damned needle."

"No heroics, Love. This is a quick grab-and-go." Kalen's voice was smooth as warm molasses and just as sweet. Damn, if he could bottle it, she'd be able to build a whole new research facility... or three. Abby didn't want to turn her back on Lamb, but she knew better than to face him. The minute he got a good look at her, David Lamb would realize she wasn't Paris.

"Paris, what the hell are you doing? Come on, sweetheart, let's get out of here."

So, that's the way he was going to play it? Make Paris feel guilty for being on Ian McGregor's infamous island? *What an asshat.*

"Go away, David. I'm not going anywhere with you. What makes you think you can come here and make demands after what happened in California?" Abby heard groans on the other end when her brother and husbands realized what she was up to, but the only one who spoke was Ian.

"Clever girl. If he incriminates himself, it'll be a huge bargaining chip, Abby."

She smiled to herself at the note of pride she heard in

Ian's voice. Ian McGregor had always been one of her biggest supporters. Hell, he'd personally funded her first lab, sending all the equipment he'd found on her online wish list to her home in Texas when he learned her parents weren't going to give her the thousands of dollars she'd requested.

It had also been Ian who'd overseen her medical care when she'd blown out a knee. Of course, Ian had used the opportunity to have the surgeon implant a third tracker— one only he or her brother could authorize activating. She'd been both furious and grateful when the small device saved her life a couple of years earlier.

Lamb's footsteps were getting closer, she didn't have much time to extract information.

"You'll drop the charges after we spend a month in Fiji. You'll see, I just got ahead of myself. I love you, and I've wanted you for so long."

He was getting too close. She had to turn, despite knowing what he'd said probably wasn't enough to secure a conviction. Facing him, Abby was startled to find him already pulling the small syringe from his pocket.

"What the fuck is that? You better put that away right now." Abby thought he'd know immediately he had the wrong woman, but David Lamb's eyes were unfocused and dilated so wide, there was no doubt he was higher than a damned kite.

"Paris Adler, you better clean up your language, or mother is going to be pissed. She's already mad at you for the stink you caused in California. Damn, she ranted about how ungrateful you are for days."

He was waving the syringe in the air like a wild man...

hell, there was no reasoning with someone in this state. Taking two quick steps back, Abby was startled by the crack of a rifle, followed immediately by a shower of rocks and leaves.

"Holy fuck. What the hell? How did you do that? God-freaking-damn it, that fucking hurts." Another crack and rocks flew everywhere, but this time, Abby was already crouching behind a low rock wall. Peeking over the upper edge, she watched Lamb dancing in place, bleeding from several gashes on backs of his bare legs. The back of his shirt was shredded and quickly becoming soaked in blood. Even from this distance, she could see none of the injuries were life-threatening, but he was going to be sore as hell for a while.

Abby knew where Logan was positioned, and the shots hadn't come from his direction. Laughing when she realized Lilly was playing with Lamb, she ducked her head, just in time to avoid being blasted by shards of rock. The third shot was closer, and he must have finally figured it out because he dropped to his knees, then fell face forward in surrender.

"Stand down, Lilly. Nice shooting by the way."

Abby could hear Jace's laughter and breathed a sigh of relief. Tony was already cuffing Lamb. He must have stepped forward a split second too soon because he had a couple of lacerations to his forearms Abby suspected were going to require stitches. Watching Tony lift Lamb roughly to his feet, she could sense his frustration. No doubt the former SEAL had been looking forward to exacting a bit of justice before turning Lamb over to the authorities, and now he was going to need to provide first aid. Yep, Lilly

West had beaten one of the country's best to the punch.

"THIRTEEN POINT THREE seconds start to finish. Damn, darlin' that new rifle Ian gave you might not be all it's cracked up to be." Del's teasing voice sounded from her left as Lilly quickly disassembled the M82 Barret 50 caliber rifle. She was in love with the gift Ian McGregor had delivered to her room early this morning.

Last night, after it was decided Lilly would be part of the team, Ian had assured her there would be a weapon in her hands before eight a.m. the following morning. She'd answered the door for the delivery at seven fifteen. *Remarkable*. She didn't know how he'd managed it, but she was damned impressed, and beyond grateful he'd gotten it done.

When her sons insisted she not be armed, Lilly had quickly reminded them she was an adult woman who made her own damned decisions. It's too bad her sons weren't as wise as her husbands.

"It's brand new. Hell, she did exactly what Ian asked her to do without a practice session." Dean gave her ass a gentle caress and grinned. "I think we should celebrate, darlin'." She couldn't hold back her snicker, but before she could respond, all three of their phones pinged with incoming messages.

Conference room in five. So much for celebrating.

Chapter Nineteen

T RINITY LOOKED DOWN at the sleeping beauty in his arms and smiled. He still marveled at how quickly his anger at her blatant disregard for the posted speed limits had morphed to ire the first time they met. The realization his mate had endangered herself made him see red. He'd been furious as he'd walked up alongside her car after pulling her over for speeding.

He'd played hell catching her. After meeting her speeding sportscar on the small two-lane highway near the outer edge of the small town his pack called home, his radar had alarmed immediately, but by the time he'd been able to turn around, Paris' rental had been little more than a speck on the horizon. She'd been close to the clinic by the time he'd caught up with her.

One whiff was all it had taken for him to recognize her. Their first meeting had been all about fireworks, but not the kind he'd always envisioned when he'd dreamed of finding his mate. Hell, who was he kidding? Paris Adler was going to be fireworks forever, and he wouldn't have it any other way.

Their flight home had been uneventful compared to what he'd heard had taken place back at Club Isola. David

Lamb had been treated at a local hospital after being arrested for unlawful entry and threatening a guest. Abby managed to get some information, but no one was convinced it would be enough to persuade the D. A. in California to take Paris' case to court. Sighing, he brushed a stray lock of hair back from her face, content to hold her while one of Eli's drivers drove them back to Paris' new home.

She didn't know her condo in California had been packed and moved while they'd been in Washington. It had cost Trinity a small fortune, but he'd managed to get all her personal belongings moved. Under the direction of his mate's sister, London, everything had already been put away. When Trinity was convinced the situation with Lamb was completely resolved, they'd discuss her moving into his home.

Only a few people knew about the tunnel connecting his palatial home with the pack headquarters—in fact, very few people outside the pack knew the timber and glass mansion overlooking the wooded area behind the clinic existed. Shaking off the direction his thoughts had taken, he pushed aside everything but his concerns for his mate's safety.

"Baby, are you going to be able to walk inside?" He wasn't surprised when she didn't so much as stir. She'd been restless on the plane, tossing and turning without the physical connection of being held. She never rested well unless she was in his arms, and it pleased him to know she felt safe in the one place she should always find solace.

Since she was technically still recovering from her head injury and needed to rest as much as possible, Trinity had forgone the seat belt to hold her on his lap during the short trip from the airport. Hopefully, the generous tip he'd given the young shifter called out in the middle of the night would keep him from sharing that juicy tidbit about the local sheriff.

Stepping out of the Towne car's backseat, his sleeping mate cradled in his arms, Trinity felt the hair on the back of his neck stand on end, just as Paris stiffened. Letting out a low growl, Paris launched herself out of his arms. Shifting in midair, she landed in a crouch in front of him as the shredded remnants of her clothing floated to the ground around them. She skirted a large hedge he knew concealed a cobblestone walkway around the house. The few seconds he'd lost in confusion turned out to be more significant than he could have ever imagined.

"Hello, Sheriff." Turning to his left, Trinity watched Senator Nancy Lamb step around a small evergreen, a small caliber handgun in her hand. *Hell*. One of Trinity's gifts was reading people, and Senator Lamb was two-and-a-half gallons of crazy in a gallon bucket—things were about to get messy. It was painfully obvious the woman wasn't comfortable or familiar with the weapon she had pointed at his chest. In his experience, an untrained person was the most dangerous person in the world when armed.

"Senator. How did you manage to skirt Dr. Monroe's security?" Her eyes lit with amusement, making her look as certifiable as the energy surrounding.

"One of my staff had an unfortunate accident early this morning. Ironically, it occurred right after my son was injured while trying to find help on a small island off the coast of our nation's capital. Amazing coincidence, don't you think?"

Oh, hell no, there wasn't anything coincidental about this at all. The only question was, how had she managed to get someone admitted to Evan's clinic so quickly?

"Let's cut to the chase, shall we? I want to speak to Paris Adler." Senator Lamb's voice went from phony sweet to ice cold so quickly, it sent chills up Trinity's spine.

"Not going to happen, Senator. You might as well tuck that pistol back in your Gucci bag and make your way down to D.C." Glancing down, Trinity noted the shattered tracking bracelet Paris had been wearing. She hadn't had time to activate the panic alarm, but he knew the failsafe had kicked in when the circuit was broken.

Trinity had personally locked the bracelet around her wrist and had the only key to open it without triggering an alarm. His phone was vibrating in his pocket, and he knew Ian's team was already responding. The damned woman who'd given birth to the Devil's spawn stalking his mate had managed to catch him without a weapon. *She'd better enjoy this moment because it was a mistake I'll never make again.*

"I'll bet she'll come back outside if she knows your life depends on it." Waving her free hand toward the clothing remnants at his feet, she added, "The little tramp is probably looking for something to wear. What did she do, rip off her clothes, trying to tempt you as she did my son?" Trinity heard the low-pitched growl behind the senator but knew the woman was unaware she was being stalked by the woman she'd just insulted.

Shifters who didn't grow up with the ability didn't understand the energy backlash associated with their first attacks. A young shifter learned those lessons over time, but a new shifter didn't have the benefit of the same exposure to the learning curve. Trinity wanted to do anything he could to keep Paris from experiencing the negative surge of energy that always followed attacking an opponent. Counting the seconds he knew it would take his deputies and the pack's security team to arrive, Trinity knew his best hope was to stall.

"Why the urgency, Senator? It seems you have gone to extraordinary lengths to talk to a woman you clearly don't like." Rocking back on his heels to distract her from the half-step he planned to take forward, Trinity tilted his head to the side, hoping she'd fall for the faux interest.

"My son has been in love with Paris Adler for years. She's led him on from the beginning." The disdain in her voice was competing with the crazy, and the combination was worrisome. The woman was pushing Paris' buttons without knowing her target was listening.

Don't let her get to you, baby. She's nuts. Scent her. Smell the difference as she gets closer and closer to the emotional edge. Let the men who are on their way do their jobs.

Trinity felt Paris' distraction and wondered who the hell she was talking to. Goddess above, this was shaping up to be a fuck-up of epic proportions. A crazy politician holding a gun she obviously had no idea how to handle safely, a new shifter with a fucking head injury who was talking to something or someone he couldn't see or hear, and a team of security personnel closing in from all sides. Yes, indeed—a recipe for disaster.

PARIS DIDN'T GIVE a rat's ass about the venom Nancy Lamb was spewing about her. Hell, she'd disliked Paris from the first time they met, why would her opinion matter now? It was the woman's malicious intent she was reacting to.

One moment, Paris had been sleeping peacefully in Trinity's arms, the next she'd been slammed with the most overwhelmingly negative energy she'd ever experienced. She hadn't thought, she'd just shifted and run for a strategic position. Her only concern was for her mate. The damned woman was pointing a gun at Trinity... what the ever-loving hell was she thinking? Paris felt her anger spike, as red-tinged her peripheral vision.

My sweet, Paris. Wait. Dad and I are here, and we'll protect your mate. If you act, we'll be forced to choose, and we'll always protect our own.

She felt a gentle hand brush over the top of her head, a soft caress she might have mistaken for a breeze if she hadn't heard her mom's voice so clearly in her mind. Her entire life, Paris had heard her parents' assurances her gifts were waiting, but until this moment, she hadn't really believed.

Never doubt your gifts, sweetheart. You were our youngest, but in so many ways, we saved the most significant bits of magic for you.

It warmed her heart to hear the love in her father's voice; it didn't matter she was hearing with her mind rather than her ears. If this was a part of the Universe's gift to her, Paris was going to consider herself incredibly blessed.

Your dad is right, baby girl. Your gifts are greater than your wildest imagination. All you have to do is step out of your own way.

In the back of her mind, Paris could hear Trinity telling her to hold her position, but she had trouble maintaining the connection to her mate because the love she felt flowing from her parents was a powerful connection she didn't want to let go.

DR. EVAN MONROE was too stunned to respond. The young woman he'd operated on an hour ago was spinning a tale so far beyond his imagination, at first, he'd assumed she'd been over-medicated. She hadn't required general anesthesia for the simple procedure, but he quickly flipped through her chart, checking to see what she'd been given since he'd left her a couple of hours earlier.

"I want you to repeat that for me, please, because what I heard was you were pushed down the stairs by a United States Senator for the sole purpose of getting into my clinic."

"Yes. She promised to pay off my student loans and give me a hundred grand bonus if I kept quiet." The young woman's eyes widened as realization dawned on her. "Oh shit, I bet I just screwed that up, huh? Damn. Now I have hardware in my ankle and no money. Wait. Maybe you could keep this quiet? Like a secret. It's a lot of money. We could pretend this conversation never happened."

Not a chance in hell.

"Do you know why Senator Lamb wanted inside the

secured perimeter of this facility?" *Swear to Goddess if she knew and helped set this up, I'll call the FBI myself.*

"Nope. She wouldn't tell me. Just kept saying she needed to get inside to talk to a girl. She's always trying to find her creepy son a girlfriend, so I figured she had her eye on one of your nurses or something. The Senator is a little crazy where her son is concerned."

Oh, Evan agreed the senator was crazy all right, but there was nothing *little* about it. Activating the recording equipment in the small recovery room, Evan moved into camera range. He'd try to get the story again, this time for the record. If Senator Lamb had injured a woman for the sole purpose of stalking Evan's sister-in-law, she had a lot to answer for.

"Okay, let's go over this one more time. I want to make certain you are receiving the best possible care. Tell me your name and what you remember about your accident." To his amazement, she gave him a verbatim recount of the story she'd recounted minutes earlier. Evan didn't believe for a minute Nancy Lamb would have kept her end of the bargain—the paper trail would have been too revealing.

I'm already on it, brother.

Evan breathed a sigh of relief, knowing his connection to his brother was strong enough to have alerted Eli to his need for help. Their world revolved around their wife, London, and that meant her sister was theirs as well. There were few places the sense of family and group loyalty were stronger than a pack of shifters.

Evan wasn't sure what was going on at his former home behind the clinic but sensed Trinity's trepidation.

Every member of the pack knew better than to communicate telepathically with Sheriff Stone when he was working unless it was a matter of life and death. Distracting him could well be the difference between the man living or dying.

"So, which one of your nurses is Nasty Nancy trying to hook up with her son? Where she'd get off to, anyway? She said she would stick around. How am I supposed to get back to the hotel? I'm getting out of here soon, right? Boy oh boy, it's sweltering in here. Could you turn on a fan?"

The woman's rapid-fire questions brought him back to the moment, and he felt himself smiling at her. His assistant had only given her a mild pain killer. The nerve block they'd used during surgery would begin fading soon, and Chatty Cathy was going to need something to head off the discomfort.

"I think it's in your best interest to spend the night here. Pain management can be tricky, and since it looks like you are on your own, we don't want you trying to stay ahead of it without help." There wasn't a chance in all creation he was letting her out of here tonight. Everything he'd just told her was true. It would be irresponsible for him to release her unless he knew she had a solid support system available—which clearly wasn't the case. But there was another reason as well.

Evan wanted to make sure Senator Lamb didn't make her a victim a second time. If the ruthless lawmaker had been willing to throw a twenty-two-year-old staff member down the stairs, she'd damned well do whatever she felt was needed to ensure the woman's silence. Evan watched her struggle to keep her eyes open and smiled. His wife was dealing with the same affliction for a different reason. The sweet babies she currently cradled in her core drained her energy more often than she liked.

London's balls-to-the-wall work ethic was being challenged, but she was fighting it with everything she had. Keeping her from overdoing was a damned full-time job. He and Eli were happy Paris would be living so close—they were depending on her to help rein in her workaholic sister.

"I think I'm supposed to protest, but I'm having trouble remembering what I'm not supposed to be happy about. My ankle hurts. I'm just going to take a little nap and hope it's better when I wake up."

It will be. My staff will make sure you sleep comfortably. Every doctor worth his salt knew pain management is second only to infection control when it comes to post-surgical healing. Patients who are fighting pain don't rest properly, their bodies focused on the pain rather than healing.

Cutting off the recording device, Evan quickly entered his medical notes in the network, then sent a message to the control center, requesting the security video be backed up and forwarded to a short list of recipients. He didn't want to take any chances and getting it into multiple hands was cheap insurance against a single file being accidentally erased. It was up to Trinity to forward the information to the FBI, but Evan intended to make certain he got the chance.

Great grab, brother, but you are not going to fucking believe what just went down at your old place. Paris just saved Trinity's life, but it looks like you're going to be working for a while. I'll keep our lovely wife occupied while you fix Senator Lamb's broken forearm.

Broken forearm? You're sure?

Oh yeah, we could hear the bones snap over the wind. The new outside equipment Ian designed last year is kick ass.

Great. Just fucking dandy. I'm stuck healing the bitch, and you're happy dancing about equipment.

And fucking our wife. She misses you, but I'll keep her occupied until you stumble in. The two of you can take a nice long nap.

There was no jealousy between them where London was concerned because they shared two all-important goals—keeping their wife safe and happy. But that didn't mean they didn't enjoy teasing each other. Eli's duties as the pack's primary Alpha usually kept him busy most of the day, whereas Evan's peak work hours were often started in the late evening. Sports enthusiasts, tired after a full day's activities, rarely had the good sense to stop before having an accident.

Their divergent schedules meant one of them was usually available to spend time with London, the caveat was, she probably wasn't getting enough rest—so the nap might be a bigger blessing than he'd first thought. Walking down the hall to the clinic's emergency room, Evan shook his head. Who was he kidding? A nap wasn't anywhere on the list of ways he'd planned to spend his time with London. His brother's laughter moved through his mind, making Evan snarl an expletive that would have had his mother batting the back of his head.

TRINITY LEANED AGAINST the marble counter in the master bath, watching Paris fight through the emotions he'd hoped to help her avoid. He'd foreseen a flash of violence seconds before Senator Lamb raised her weapon. Time seemed to slow when he saw the finger she'd kept on the trigger flex in anticipation. It hadn't been difficult to calculate the angle of her weapon and know she was aiming dead center at his heart. Had she made the shot, he wouldn't be standing here now.

Paris' lightning-fast reaction gave him the fraction of a second he'd needed to launch himself to the side, avoiding the shot. The gun's sharp retort bounced off the home's stone façade, echoing between the house and clinic—hell, his ears had rung for almost an hour. His mate hadn't taken the woman apart, but the power of her jaws had broken both bones in the woman's arm. He wondered how the Senator's public relations team was going to explain their boss's wild ramblings about being bitten by a wolf. It wouldn't matter it was the truth, no one was going to believe her outrageous claim.

It was damned hard to stand back watching his sweet mate suck in shuddering breaths as she battled her way back from the tsunami of emotions moving through her. As much as he looked forward to comforting her, he knew these few seconds were about letting Paris get her feet back under her. Trinity knew his sweet mate was worried about the stark differences in their life experience, so he planned to empower her at every turn.

Until she understood her own worth, he'd keep reminding her—and right now, that meant giving her time to reclaim some of her inner strength. He watched as her spine straightened, her shoulders rolled back, the sound of her pulling in a steadying breath was music to his ears. *And there she is—the fierce woman I see every time I look at my mate.* Striping out of his clothes, Trinity moved into the shower. Pulling her back against his front, he didn't speak for several seconds, wanting to offer his silent support until he knew she was ready for the words.

"Thank you." He gave her a gentle squeeze letting her know he'd heard and understood her whispered words. "I appreciate you giving me a chance to pull myself together. My siblings always wanted to slay my dragons... but I'm grateful you let me do it. You let me prove to myself I could." Turning in his arms, she pressed her cheek against his chest, making him thankful he'd had the insight to hold back.

"You are so much stronger than you know, baby. Hell, you saved my life. I'd hoped to spare you that negative backwash of energy, but you managed a level of restraint most lifelong shifters would have found difficult to pull off." While he spoke, Trinity started shampooing her hair. When she rubbed her pebbled nipples against him, he growled. "Don't start something you're not ready to finish baby, because there's nothing I'd like better than to lift you against the wall and bury my cock in your sweet heat." Inhaling, he smiled down at her. "Fuck, you smell delicious. Change of plans." Before she could respond, he set her on the edge of the bench and sealed his mouth over her sex.

Skipping the preliminaries wasn't his usual style, but he wanted her to feel how desperately he wanted her. Rolling his tongue, Trin speared it deep into her core, flicking the tip over her opening then along her vaginal walls. Damn, she was already close, her sweet honey tempting him to push her over.

"Give it to me, Paris. Your releases belong to your Dom." He'd barely finished the command when her entire body arched, a rush of her cream coating his tongue. Trinity heard his own growl as her flavor was further imprinted on his soul. Fucking hell, she was something. "One more, baby." Biting down gently on her pretty pink pearl, Paris' wail was the sweetest sound he'd ever heard.

"Please. Oh, Goddess, please fuck me, Master. I... need you."

Trinity smiled against the swollen tissues of her sex. His sweet mate didn't hesitate to profess her love but still struggled to admit how much she craved the freedom she found in his dominance. Moving back, Trinity rose to his feet. Looking down into her confused expression, he kept his own neutral. *It's time to up the stakes, sweet sub.*

"Stand up." When she finally managed to stand, he nodded his approval. Hell, Trinity knew she was running on fumes, her knees wobbling slightly, but she recovered quickly, so he continued. "Turn around, grasp the edge of the bench." Her movements weren't well-practiced, but that was to be expected. Paris wasn't a trained submissive, and the past few months had been harrowing for her. She was right, she needed him—but not for the reasons she believed. Pushing her feet further apart, he slipped the tips of his fingers through her wet, silky folds.

"Fucking hell, you are perfect. I'm looking forward to bending you over every available surface, baby. It will give me great joy to pose you for my viewing pleasure." Having her bent over, her sex exposed while he watched a movie was a fantasy he planned to fulfill, sooner rather than later. When he saw her sway, he knew it was time to give them both the relief they needed. One push and he was buried so deep, he felt his tip pressing against her cervix. The searing heat of her vagina, the rippling of the muscles lining the walls, and the slick honey coating his cock pushed his control to the snapping point.

"So good. The sweet burning from the way your cock stretches me... Oh, Goddess, it's so good." He loved how she'd learned to express herself during sex. There were many Doms at the club who required their subs to remain silent, but Trinity loved hearing how affected his little sub was by his touch.

"You're killing me, baby." Pumping his hips in irregularly timed thrusts, Trinity focused on keeping them both on their feet as a release—so strong, it felt like a runaway train—blindsided him. "Come for me, mate. You belong to me Paris, just as I belong to you."

Trinity knew he would remember this moment until his dying day. This coupling had been so much more than sex between a Dom and sub. The searing deep in his chest felt as if their souls had just melded together—reminding him of the stories he'd read in the ancient manuscripts. Their descriptions had always sounded sappy and overly romanticized, but now... for the first time, he understood.

Leaning down, he pressed his tongue against the two small scars from their mating. The intimacy of the touch sent Paris over again, this time her knees folded out from under her he'd been ready.

With David and Nancy Lamb both out of commission

for the foreseeable future, Trinity looked forward to helping his mate settle into her new life. He didn't expect smooth sailing. If he was honest, he knew he'd be bored to distraction with a mate who was well-behaved. No worries, there. Paris Adler was going to keep him on his toes—and he wouldn't have it any other way.

Chapter Twenty

Five Months Later

PARIS LOOKED AROUND the elaborately decorated pool area, so giddy with excitement, she was practically bouncing on the balls of her feet. The friends she'd made four months ago at Club Isola had already landed at the airport the Monroe pack recently built a few miles from the clinic and would be arriving in the next few minutes. She looked forward to seeing them again and enjoying the margarita party they'd missed when she'd fallen. The party had been tweaked a bit to accommodate a surprise baby shower they'd somehow managed to keep secret from her sister, London.

The doctors were still raving about the remarkable recovery Paris made during her overnight hospital stay. Since none of them knew she'd been mated with a shifter, their awe was easy to understand. One of the most remarkable things about shifters was their ability to heal at such a greatly accelerated rate. Aside from the night she'd saved Trinity's life, Paris had only been able to shift on nights when the moon was full and the sky clear. Several of the pack elders insisted the ability would strengthen with time.

Paris refused to worry about something she couldn't control; it was a non-issue as far as she was concerned.

"I swear I'd slap that smug look off your face if I could get my whale ass out of this chair." It was hard to take London's comment too seriously when she was failing miserably to hold back a fit of giggles. "A margarita party? Really, Paris? What the holy hell possessed you to do this to me? You couldn't wait for another... well, okay... I get that another fourteen months seems like a long time, but still."

"Well, since you're still a couple of months from delivering those sweet babies, then we need to add on a whole year of breastfeeding, it adds up quickly. And let's face it, your men are going to be trying to knock you up again at the first opportunity, so I decided to take your reproductive schedule off my party-planning check-list."

"Bitch."

Her sister's snark didn't fool Paris. London was thrilled to be starting her family. Paris had never seen her sister happier, her transition to working a fraction of her former sixty hours a week hadn't been as smooth as her husbands would have liked, but it had been a walk in the park compared to what Paris expected, so she assured them it was a win.

"Don't be ugly. You don't see me complaining about you kicking back, playing relaxed lady of leisure like you were born to the role." Paris barely managed to dodge the cloth napkin London threw at her. "Be nice, or I'll tell your children how wretched their mother treated their favorite aunt."

London's eyes filled with tears, and Paris smiled at her

indulgently. Damn, her sister had been riding this emotional roller coaster for so long, Paris worried she was never going to be on an even keel again. *Who knew people actually cried while watching beer commercials? She's probably going to need counseling. Geez.*

She'll be fine, baby. Her men are watching her closely. Trinity's words moved silently through her mind making her sigh with contentment. It had taken her a couple of months to adjust to telepathic communication, but once she'd learned to block a few of her thoughts, allowing her the illusion of privacy, she'd come to appreciate the intimate connection.

"Are you pleased it's Christmas break at the school?" London's question brought Paris back to the moment.

"Not really. I'm going to miss the students, but I'm glad Bliss agreed to come today." Hiring Bliss Turner was hands down one the best decisions Paris and the Pack Council had made. She was enthusiastic about educating the group's children in a place where they didn't have to worry about keeping their lives outside school completely secret.

As a shifter, Bliss understood how difficult traditional schools were for the pack's little ones, and her vision for where the school should be in five years was perfectly in line with the pack leaders. Bliss was incredibly compassionate, and when Abby had called asking if she knew any single women who might be a good fit for one of the Doms at Club Isola, Paris knew instinctively Bliss needed to be at this party.

"Does Trinity know you're helping Abby with her matchmaking project?" London's teasing question made

Paris grin. Her sister might think she was throwing her under the bus, but Paris knew very little escaped her mate's attention.

"Of course, he does." Trinity's deep voice sounded from over her shoulder, making Paris jump, but before she could tumble forward, he snaked his arm around her waist. "Oh no, you don't, baby. My heart can't take seeing you hurt again." She giggled as he nuzzled the tender spot below her ear. After her fall at Club Isola, Trinity's tough guy persona faded to the background unless her physical safety was at stake.

"I'm happy you thought of Bliss. To be honest, I think she and Tony would be good together. But putting them in the same space is the extent of your *help*, understood? They are adults, and they'll find each other if it's meant to be."

Paris nodded, too distracted by the warmth of his breath wafting over her skin to speak. Damn, the man was potent. There were times he didn't have to do more than wink at her, and Paris felt like she would melt into a puddle.

"Oh, Goddess. Sap Alert. Get a room already."

London's snark made Paris giggle, but before she could reply, the door burst open, her friends streaming into the room. The din of laughter made Paris' heart dance with joy. Abby carried a pink bundle in her arms, and Paris couldn't wait to meet India Garrett. She already knew the baby girl was nicknamed Indy in honor of Abby's childhood nickname for her brother, Jace. The little girl's jet-black hair and electric blue eyes made her the spitting image of Kalen Black, and Paris wondered if she'd inherit his voice as well.

"I know what you're thinking," Abby giggled and shook her head. "You'll find out as soon as she's hungry, her voice is anything but angelic. I have no idea where she gets it, but she is *loud*." Paris burst into giggles at Abby's obvious sarcasm. They'd stayed in touch over the past few months. Abby had even agreed to visit the school before the end of the term to speak to the female students about the importance of science and math.

As more guests arrived, the pile of gifts mounting, London was no longer fooled. By the end of the evening, Paris had laughed so hard, her sides ached. Looking around her, she sent up a silent prayer of gratitude. She was safe. Both Senator and David Lamb seemed to have lost interest in her after the District Attorney in California failed to take her case to trial. She was surrounded by friends, she had a job she loved, and a mate she loved more every day.

Now... if Bliss and the Dom from Club Isola would show up and fall in love, things would be pretty close to perfect.

Epilogue

Tony Dent followed a small car up the driveway, marveling the small bucket of bolts was moving under its own power. He wasn't sure he'd ever seen a car with more dents and scrapes outside of a demolition derby. The light smattering of snow wasn't enough to cause his rental any trouble, but the little car ahead of him was slipping side to side with alarming frequency. Whoever had braved this trek in that car deserved a fucking friendship trophy.

When the car finally slid to a stop, he watched in amused horror as an enormous puff of black smoke billowed from the tattered tailpipe. Holy fuck, it wasn't until the car shuddered to a stop, he realized how loud it had been. Jesus, Joseph, and sweet mother Mary, the driver's ears had to be ringing. Stepping out of the truck he'd picked up at the airport, Tony's attention was drawn to the jalopy's driver. He'd missed her exit, but there was no missing the spectacular ass pointed his way. She was bent over retrieving a package from the backseat, oblivious to the strange man standing behind her.

When she stood, he saw her eyes widen in surprise before flaring with something he was sure was sexual interest.

The moment of barely restrained sensual awareness morphed to alarm when she took a step forward. Before Tony could move to her side, the woman's arms were pinwheeling as she crashed to the ground. He was crouched beside her before she could scramble to her feet.

"Oh, Goddess, this is so embarrassing. Just once, I'd like to meet someone and not fall on my tush. It's humiliating... predictable, but still disconcerting. Being a klutz sucks, I tell you. I'll bet you don't have this trouble."

"Nope. Not unless I put my leg on backward. I have to admit, that makes navigating pretty damned challenging." Her expression went from embarrassed to something close to awe in the blink of an eye.

"You can put your leg on backward?" He didn't detect anything other than interest in her voice, so he plunged ahead. *Might as well put it out there and save it being an issue later.*

"Not really. I was teasing, but I do put one of them on every morning thanks to an IED on the other side of the planet a few years ago."

"Wow. I'm humbled. Your reactions were so quick and knowing you had such a devastating injury... and as a.... umm, teacher, I'm supposed to be graceful." He hadn't made it to her side in time to keep her from falling, but he'd been at her side within a fraction of a second.

"Teachers are supposed to be graceful?" *Poor little shifter doesn't know Ian updated me on the Monroe pack's secret.*

"Is your leg one of those high-tech ones? I'll bet it allows you to do all sorts of things. I had a friend in college who lost her leg in a car accident. She went through several different prostheses before she finally got one she liked, but she hung in there."

Tony blinked several times, trying to take in everything about the sweet woman staring up at him in excitement. He'd never met anyone outside the medical community with previous experience in prosthetics.

"Can you swim with yours? How about skiing? Biking? Tessa could do it all, it was impressive."

When she finally paused long enough to take a breath, he wondered if she'd back off like all the others. He knew she'd misinterpreted his silence when the tone of her voice changed from excited to apologetic.

"I'm sorry if I'm too forward, but you seemed open to talking about it... and I don't get to talk to many adults. I guess I got carried away." She cast her eyes down as her cheeks flushed the prettiest pink Tony had seen in a long time. *I wonder if she knows she's a sub?*

"Sweetness, I'm always open to talking about my new leg. And yes, it's high tech. The man I work for is a techno genius, and I've been testing all his newest improvements to the prosthesis. He's changing everything about them. Your friend is going to be thrilled when his products hit the market."

"Really? Oh, that's terrific. Can you tell me anything about them, or is it a secret? I'd love to learn more. Are you going to Paris' party? Oh. Are you, umm... friends?"

For the first time, he saw a hint of hesitation. *Interesting. She wants to make sure I'm not here to see her friend.* Loyalty was a damned appealing trait, and Tony felt his cock stir as interest flared deep in his core.

Holding out his hand to shake hers, Tony smiled. "Paris and I have mutual friends—that's how I scored an invitation to the party." And I'm suddenly very happy I decided to make the trip. "My name is Tony Dent." When she placed her hand in his, Tony swore he felt a jolt of electricity race up his arm.

"It's nice to meet you, Tony, I'm Bliss Turner. Paris and I work together." *Bliss.* For the first time in months, Tony was looking forward to a party. Tucking her hand into the crook of his arm, Tony led her up the stone steps. He wasn't taking any chances she'd fall. Before they reached the door, she stopped suddenly, looking up at him hesitantly.

"Are you okay, sweetness?"

"Would you mind terribly if we sat for just a few minutes? I promised Paris I'd come, but I'm nervous about meeting her friends... they all sound so amazing, and I'm sort of a dork." A dork? *Oh no, we aren't starting out like this, little sub.*

"You are not a dork. I'm enjoying your company, and I'd prefer you didn't refer to my new friend in a negative sense." Using the tip of his finger, he tapped the tip of her nose for emphasis. Sitting together on a rock ledge, Tony was grateful they were protected from the crisp evening breeze. The cold didn't usually bother him, but he was enjoying Bliss's company and hoped warding off the chill would encourage her to stay outside longer.

"I love the brisk night air. It's energizing."

Laughing to himself, he realized she was probably more resilient to the cold than he was. Damn, she was intriguing. He'd never wanted to be in a long-distance relationship, but he might have to rethink things. Maybe— just maybe he'd found a woman who wouldn't fuck him for the freak factor then walk away. Listening to Bliss marvel at the beauty of the darkening night sky, Tony grinned when he realized they were both looking at something beautiful. Her slender face was turned up to the heavens, but he was focused on her.

He'd suspected Abby was matchmaking when she'd invited him, but decided to attend, anyway, needing an excuse to get away from work for a few days. He hoped there wasn't a woman inside waiting to meet him because he had no intention of letting go of the one sitting beside him until they'd explored the attraction flaring between them. Laughing to himself, Tony couldn't help but wonder. Hell, knowing Abby, she'd arranged for them to arrive at the same time—yep, the new mama was that good.

The End

Books by Avery Gale

The Adlers
Brooklyn
London
Austin
Paris

The ShadowDance Club
Katarina's Return – Book One
Jenna's Submission – Book Two
Rissa's Recovery – Book Three
Trace & Tori – Book Four
Reborn as Bree – Book Five
Red Clouds Dancing – Book Six
Perfect Picture – Book Seven

Club Isola
Capturing Callie – Book One
Healing Holly – Book Two
Claiming Abby – Book Three

Masters of the Prairie Winds Club
Out of the Storm
Saving Grace
Jen's Journey
Bound Treasure
Punishing for Pleasure
Accidental Trifecta
Missionary Position
Another Second Chance
Star-Crossed Miracles
Dusted Star
Lilly's Choice

The Wolf Pack Series
Mated – Book One
Fated Magic – Book Two
Tempted by Darkness – Book Three

The Knights of the Boardroom
Book One
Book Two
Book Three

The Morgan Brothers of Montana
Coral Hearts – Book One
Dancing with Deception – Book Two
Caged Songbird – Book Three
Game On – Book Four
Well Bred – Book Five

Mountain Mastery
Well Written
Savannah's Sentinel
Sheltering Reagan

The Christmas Painting
Taking Out the Mother of the Bride

I would love to hear from you!

Email: avery.gale@ymail.com

Website: www.averygale.com

Facebook: facebook.com/avery.gale.3

Twitter: @avery_gale